# CRUMPETS

HOWARD G AWBERY

Published by New Generation Publishing in 2024

First Edition

ISBN: 978-1-83563-467-7

**www.newgeneration-publishing.com**

New Generation Publishing

*To Will,*
*I just hope you felt I was half as good a friend to you*
*as you were to me.*

# CRUMPETS

# 1

It was Saturday evening and everything in the street was painted gloomy grey. Relentless rain compounded the dismal scene; rain that even the most excitable of dogs reject when their owners try to coax them out for a walk. This forgotten Victorian street, just off the High Street in South London, looked as wet and dank as it could, presenting a November welcome that bordered on hostile to strangers. The only activity was an ageing Citroen 2CV, with wobbly headlights, creeping forwards and backwards close to the pavement.

"Number 46-48-50-54. I told you so last time. There's no number 52 Bucket Street," complained Dave as he feigned interest while peering into the dark. The windscreen wipers, nearing the end of their life, flopped wearily back and forth making little impression on the flat screen. Dave half-heartedly rubbed the inside of the passenger window with his coat sleeve, making things worse by smearing the opaque glass.

Once again, Emma noisily clonked the protesting gear lever into reverse and began edging the car backwards. Her visibility out of the back window was nil so she was reversing by ear, listening for the scraping of her wheel hubs on the granite curb.

There definitely was a 56 Bucket Street; the number was nailed drunkenly above the completely boarded over front door. Steel mesh doubled as curtains. It was an early 1900s terraced house whereas 54 Bucket Street was a butcher's shop. Eerie blue lights flickered in the meat display counter, chilling any welcome. 50 Bucket Street was a dying newsagent's shop complete with peeling, faded adverts obscuring both windows. An overflowing waste bin was chained to the shop front wall and a growing pile of rubbish, obviously thrown in its general direction, surrounded it on the floor. The chained waste bin said it all about Bucket Street.

Not a single light in any of the windows of the Bucket Street houses was visible from the street. In fact, there weren't any lights evident in any of the houses, upstairs or downstairs; on either side of the street. A fact noted by Emma, but chosen to be ignored. Both sides of the street were lit by murky, yellow, sodium lamps and lights bolted onto house fronts. Some were lit, some were not, some were flashing in their death throes. Thirty years ago, these lights would have been considered state-of-the-art, but today, compared with the recently installed bright lights at the High Street end of the street, the best of these sodium lights was discouragingly dim. The long, dark, unlit stretches would discourage any footfall along the miserable street after sunset, Emma silently observed.

She turned her attention back to the search in hand. Upon further examination, nestled between the butcher's and newsagent's shops, but completely obscured by graffiti covered boarding that morphed into the brickwork, a concealed door was tucked. A corner of it was all that could be seen between the two equally well boarded adjacent windows of the shop for sale. It all had to be number 52 Bucket Street. It couldn't be anything else.

Emma squealed with delight, making Dave jump when she spotted it. However, there was no distinguishing name or number. There was nothing distinguishing about it at all. In fact, it gave the distinct impression to the world that it did not want to be found! Number 52 Bucket Street appeared content to remain inconspicuous to the point of being invisible.

The brakes jolted the little car to a sudden stop and Emma turned, scrabbling to find the estate agent's blurb on the cluttered back seat. She twisted the paper this way and that, trying to see in the six-volt interior light of the car.

She read aloud, "A traditional feature entrance to a double-fronted shop. This highly sought-after premises has the potential to become, with imagination, a high turnover retail outlet." Emma looked out, trying to reconcile the poetic description with what she saw.

"Who writes this bollocks?" snapped Dave. He followed with a plea, "Come on, Em, the whole street's a dog hole. We can't leave the car unattended 'cos we'll come back to it balancing on bricks. There's no way I want to see inside that grotty building and what's more, Chelsea is playing Man U in twenty minutes at 7.00 pm in the semi-final of the Cup Winners' Cup. I've seen every Cup Winners' Cup, evening, semi-final for ten years and I don't want 1990 to be the first match I've missed. So come on, Em, I've set up the beers and the crisps and our shirts are already on the back of our chairs."

"Now we've found it, I'd at least like to have a look inside," countered Emma.

"Inside! Oh, now you must be joking, Em. If we leave now, we could just get home for the kick-off. I've been looking forward to the match all week," he pleaded. "How about we call for fish, chips, mushy peas and lashings of gravy on the way home? My treat." He exaggerated the description about lashings of gravy, believing the treat would be irresistible to Emma.

However, Emma was already out of the car and tugging at the camouflaging timber boarding as his inducement tailed off to the drumming of the rain on the ancient car's soft-top.

"Come on, Dave, help me," she excitedly implored. "I'm sure we can do this."

A very reluctant Dave shrugged his shoulders, pulled up his collar, stepped out onto the wet road, slammed the flimsy car door shut and unenthusiastically shuffled over to the boarded-up shop front. He put his fingers behind the old plywood boards, swollen by decades of weather, and heaved. After two or three pulls the first board came off. Once the first board was off, the rest were relatively easy to remove.

They stacked the wet boards on the pavement and examined the door, looking for the lock. After brushing away donkeys' years of dust and grime, the half-filled-in keyhole became visible. However, to make matters worse, despite Emma's best efforts, the old Yale lock seemed to be unyielding.

The rain increased its onslaught on the pair, further dampening Dave's spirits. He became more and more frustrated as the soggy minutes to kick-off sped by.

"He's given us the wrong bloody key for God's sake. Estate agents, what a waste of space," finally exploded an exasperated Dave. "Let's go home, Em. I'm soaked right through to my pants!"

"No, I've nearly done it."

Emma's key wiggling persistence paid off and it eventually turned. She edged the door inwards half an inch and it immediately wedged against what she presumed to be a mountain of circulars, ancient yellowing telephone directories and aged post. It felt like the shop's last-ditch barricade to keep them out, a last desperate effort to retain its isolation, allowing it to slumber back for many more years of obscurity.

Emma wasn't disillusioned though, and after much cajoling she managed to persuade Dave to push the obstinate door open just enough to squeeze her petite frame through. Once inside, she kicked the circulars to one side and opened the door sufficiently to let him in too. The only light, now the boards had been removed from the door and windows, came from a flashing, far-off street lamp, which didn't really help for it threw a collage of intimidating shadows across the walls. Their eyes took a few moments to become accustomed to the darkness.

Undeterred, Emma hunted for her one-lumen keyring torch. It offered just enough illumination to help her find the light switch. She beckoned Dave over.

He peered in horror at the dangling light switch and the shiny, threadbare wiring before sarcastically declaring, "Only if I was standing on two feet of rubber matting, had a ten-inch pole and was happy to die, would I be prepared to touch that switch."

Emma pushed past him and flicked it on herself.

"You really are a wuss sometimes," she said.

The single dusty light bulb lit up the room. They both looked around. Dave confirmed to himself he wasn't staying while Emma silently confirmed she was.

"Wow," said Emma. "It's so much bigger from the inside than I expected."

Dave clocked that her eyes were as wide open as he'd ever seen them.

"Forget it," he said, brushing wet hair out of his eyes, the rain off his coat and stamping his sodden feet.

Looking from the middle of the empty shop towards the front door, Emma discovered that each of the front windows were bowed outwards. Not at all the single plate glass window she'd expected. Even better, each window was made up of small square panes of glass about a foot square with the odd, round, bull's eye pane here and there.

"Come and look at these windows, Dave, they're so traditional. With the glass cleaned and the frames varnished they could look amazing," exclaimed Emma to deaf ears.

The display shelves at the base of the windows were wide enough to sit upon but obscured by piles of ancient magazines. They were yellowed with age and all their corners curled up. Emma imagined serving afternoon tea to customers sitting in the bay windows watching the world go by.

Along one side of the shop, nearly the full length of the interior was a dusty surface. Pulling a very reluctant Dave with her, Emma ran her finger in the thick dust disclosing a highly polished, conker coloured counter. She traced it the full length. Her vision of the future was in overdrive. Dave coughed at the dust.

She noticed an assortment of old chairs stacked in a corner of the room and a heap of worn-out kitchen utensils abandoned on top of some cream-coloured, low-level cupboards. Behind the counter for half its length, high wooden cupboards reached the ceiling and when she opened one, she imagined freshly washed white China cups, plates, saucers, water jugs and tiered cake stands.

Emma ignored Dave's continuous stream of derogatory remarks about the property and made her way to the back of the shop to explore further. Another suicide switch lit the back room, which was at right angles to the main shop and nearly as big. It was fitted with a large, cracked, Belfast ceramic sink and a 1950s sideboard with the left-hand door hanging from one hinge. Apart from that, the room was empty.

Emma imagined this back room as a fully furnished, brightly lit, bustling, stainless-steel kitchen. It could be fantastic. She imagined the noisy jostle of plates being stacked, of pots being washed. She could hear a stream of orders being shouted from the counter above Radio One music, could already smell bacon, see eggs sizzling and popping of hot fat and hear the coffee machine gurgling its Robusta music.

The protesting back door finally opened outwards into an unlit, dark yard full of rubbish and junk. The whole yard was surrounded by a high brick wall iced with broken glass set in cement. It was a forbidding, dark, miserable scene. Emma saw a pretty, urban garden.

"Come on, Em," implored Dave, bored out of his brains. "I've seen enough. There'll be other shops, far better than this crappy place. Let's go now!"

"Let's see what the flat's like upstairs," she replied.

"The flat? Not a chance! No way, I've seen enough. I'll be in the car, if it's still there! You must be bonkers if you want to see any more," shouted Dave crossly over his shoulder as he stomped off.

The already narrow stairs to the flat were further tapered by stacks of old books on one side of every step, leaving just enough room for a slim foot belonging to someone with advanced balance. At the top, a door opened straight into a bedroom. The half-light from the street meant Emma could just make out that the room was furnished with a painted chest of drawers, an old single bedstead and what looked like a piano stool. She walked over to the sash window and looked out; it was now raining even harder. Dave was already in the car with music blaring out. She decided, there and then, if she was to have any hope of getting him remotely interested, she would need to deploy all her womanly guile.

The bathroom and toilet were combined and very small, but surprisingly much cleaner than expected. The third room was a lounge/dining room/cupboard. It was tiny; there was barely enough room for a two-seater settee, but that and reading glasses would be all that would be required to watch TV.

Could we live here? she pondered. Could we live together in this tiny flat above the place where we worked? Would it be healthy? Would our relationship survive? Could we transform the place? Surely there's somewhere better –

there must be, she argued with herself. There probably is, but not at this price, she countered.

There was a reason why the property hadn't sold for years and it was probably down to the formidable amount of work needed as well as the run-down area. Maybe it was down to another million problems she could not even guess at yet. The low price definitely reflected the amount of work required to bring it back to life, but it was doable – just. Yet compared to trying to convince Dave to move, transforming the property would be a walk in the park.

# 2

"No, no, no, no. Not if hell had me will I leave this comfortable, clean, centrally heated spacious flat and go and live in that dog hole!" said Dave, returning his attention to the football.

"But it's the right price, it could be amazing," retorted Emma who had secretly visited the property twice more on her own in the past week.

"Emma, I don't care even if it's free! In fact, I don't care even if they paid us to live there, I'm not going. Get it? I AM NOT GOING TO LIVE THERE."

She had already used up all her womanly cunning with two large gin and tonics, his favourite dinner and a bottle of expensive red wine, but he hadn't budged an inch. Soft music, candles and the bedroom hadn't worked either. At a loss as to know what to do next, Emma was watching her dream crumble in front of her as the evening rolled on.

"Then, I'll go on my own!" There, she'd said it to the back of his head. She'd said it before she realised. She waited for the explosion.

There wasn't one. Just silence. No reaction at all, no emotion, nothing.

After a long silence, Dave switched off the TV and quietly said, "I'm going for a pint." He pulled on his coat. At the front door he turned and said, "Perhaps you should go on your own and start your café. Perhaps you going will be for the best. Perhaps you need to go and get it out of your system. I love you to bits, but I'm not going to that dreadful place." He closed the door behind him.

That was it? Three years together and that was it? Their relationship over. Her crazy dream had come between them. No row, no other woman, no illicit affair, no lipstick on his collar and no lying. Just, 'perhaps you going will be for the best'.

When he eventually came home, they talked well into the night.

Finally, he said, "I'm not leaving my good job, going to that god-forsaken building in that run-down area of town and working my ass off on your dream of a café that is doomed to fail from the start. We'll lose all our savings in the first six months and probably both end up bankrupt. And if you don't go, but stay here with me, you'll always blame me for stopping you living your dream. I'm not having that so you'd better go and do your own thing. I'll go off and do mine." Then he went to bed in the spare room. And that was that.

Emma cried the whole night through, but by morning was even more determined to make a go of her café. Deciding between her dream, her challenge, her venture with a run-down café and Dave was hard. However, she knew if she didn't do it now, she never would and she'd regret it forever. But she did love him so. Why wouldn't he just try? Why wouldn't he just try for a few months? He could be so bloody intransigent, just like his old-fashioned father.

On the other hand, she tried to give him the benefit of the doubt. Perhaps he was the one who was right? Perhaps he could see a future peppered with arguments over money and tiredness? Perhaps he knew they would clash like Titans over the running of the café, menus, opening hours, prices and customers? Maybe he was right?

No, he bloody well isn't right! Emma thought. She was right and she would have her café. She was sure she could do it... probably.

Three difficult days later and all her worldly goods were packed into, and onto, her Citron 2CV as she left to stay with a friend for a while, just till she sorted herself out.

Surrounded by boxes everywhere in her friend's tiny spare room Emma forged a plan. She needed to talk to someone who had climbed this particular mountain. Someone who would tell it as it is. That person was one of her friend's aunts. This aunt had run a beach café and offered to spend an evening with Emma, grounding her dream. The aunt talked of business plans, cash flow problems, forecasting and the like. This was a new vocabulary for Emma and made her start to wonder if she had made a mistake.

When Emma nervously explained she would be doing it all on her own as she had recently left her boyfriend the aunt snapped, "If you want a partner in business then get a dog!" Emma was taken aback by her comment. The aunt continued, "You're perfectly capable of making all the decisions yourself. You don't need a partner who you have to check with before you make a decision, especially not a man!"

The evening was exactly what Emma needed. It had knocked out of her all her doubts. She was now really fired up and ready to take on all-comers.

Shortly after leaving Dave, Emma made an offer to the solicitor acting for the property owner. It was a cheeky offer on the café, which was all she could afford without Dave's stake, at just above half the ambitious asking price.

Two days later she received a phone call from the solicitor. "As the only interested buyer for many years, the owner's response to your offer is that if you can complete the transaction in four weeks, then our client would be happy to sell the freehold on number 52 Bucket Street for that price."

Emma had whooped when the official confirmation came through, gleefully running around her friend's flat waving the letter.

However, she knew convincing the bank to loan her enough money to refurbish the shop on top of the mortgage was going to be even more challenging than Dave, but caught up in the excitement of it all, she made an appointment then set to work creating a business plan. There was no way she was falling at this initial financial hurdle.

———

A few weeks later she was the proud owner of number 52 Bucket Street and also had some money to refurbish her dream café.

Then came the day Emma excitedly took her best friends Zoe and Jinny to see it for the first time. Even before they went inside, they scanned the neighbourhood and winced on her behalf. The disbelief in their eyes as she showed them around her new venture was transparent and she could feel the glances of concern arcing between them behind her back.

Zoe was the first to speak, "The building," she hesitantly admitted, "has enormous potential, Emma, with loads of imagination and hard work."

Jinny added, "And a wand."

Zoe continued trying to get her head around the magnitude of the work. "What work will the professional builders do and what are you planning to do yourself, Em?"

Emma enthusiastically drew out on the dusty counter top the sketches of her vision for the cafe. She explained to Zoe and Jinny her ambitious timeline plans. Zoe asked a few more questions and then, out of the blue, the two of them offered to help during their two-week summer holidays, if she needed them. Emma burst into tears and hugged them both. Their offer couldn't be more timely for once the building work had been completed, the three of them were to get the café cleaned up ready for the grand opening.

"What are you going to call it, Em?" Jinny asked.

Emma beamed through her tears. "*Crumpets*," she said defiantly.

———

Sid the builder had stated there were two months of hard work required before the opening, and true to his word, he and his team arrived on the dot of 8.00 a.m. on a crisp but sunny Monday. In the process of clearing the site, three huge skips of rubbish were removed from Emma's dream café. It looked like a bombsite! She wondered if it would ever look like her vision.

However, after six weeks of round-the-clock graft, it began to take shape. It was becoming a reality. Then came the time for Zoe and Jinny to join her and they really made a difference. Working with the workmen was fun and the three friends bantered with the guys all day long. When the first oven was installed, Emma insisted on cooking everyone a full English. Without exception, they all declared *Crumpets* a huge success even as they all sat in the shavings and rubble on the floor.

————

The day of the grand opening came and *Crumpets* was heaving. The blackboard menu boasted specials in Emma's chalk handwriting. *Breakfast to go* led on to a *double full-cooked* for labourers and heavy-weight wrestlers, followed by a small range of meals with a couple of vegetarian options for lunch.

Emma gazed around the bursting café. Today had been a huge success but her mind was way ahead planning what was to be her favourite offering: *Afternoon tea* with hot crumpets, jam, cream and pots of tea. She hoped it would become her calm time of the day, the time when the elderly came to enjoy being pampered. She imagined them always being a delight to serve and always fun despite all their bunions and wonky hips. Suddenly she realised it was eighteen weeks to the day since she had left Dave which made even more proud of everything she had achieved.

Emma was brought back to earth when Zoe shouted that they were running out of bacon. The butcher offered to open up his shop and the crisis was soon solved. Oh, how she wished Dave could see it now with its bright red gingham tablecloths, polished counter top, mirrors, bright lights, shiny windows and tubs of spring flowers on both sides of the front door. Fluttering bunting hung from the upstairs windows to the furthest points of her property.

"No, she chided herself, I don't care what he thinks. He can go to hell." But she did care, although not nearly as much as she thought she would.

————

The butcher's shop next door was a very good butcher's shop, run by a young guy called Dan who, as *Crumpets* settled into its rhythm, regularly came in for coffee and toast before he opened his own shop in the morning.

The young butcher had been trained by his father, a master butcher, and they had worked together in the shop for years. Since his father's recent death, he had been running the shop single-handedly and hating every minute of it. In a low, quiet moment, he admitted to himself he wanted to call it a day. Dan's plan had been to shut up the shop one Friday evening and go travelling. Travelling to lands he had only heard of, to places he could only imagine. He wanted to meet and live amongst people who valued saner rules than Bucket Street's rules, people who lived by codes of honesty, integrity and community. People who looked after each other... because they wanted to.

Before Emma arrived, he was just making ends meet, but now he supplied *Crumpets* with all its meat requirements and encouraged every one of his customers to go next door and try the 'amazing cream tea'. Emma had turned all his travel plans upside-down and he decided to give his shop another go in the light of her arrival.

A couple of times when Emma was rushed off her feet, Dan cleared the tables and put the pots into the kitchen for her. He even encouraged some of his friends to do the same when they had finished their meals and the café was really busy. He was full of encouragement for Emma, introducing her to the locals and helping her understand the reason for some of their quaint ways.

Emma's enthusiasm had been like a breath of fresh air to the area so he started to complement her enthusiasm by cleaning up his shop front.

The two of them stood outside in the early morning air just chatting when Dan said,

"I never wanted to go into the butchery trade in the first place you know. I've always erred on the side of being a vegetarian, but family is family. Since Dad died, I've become a full vegetarian and everything to do with the trade is anathema." Dan shook his head and sighed.

Emma chose not to say anything for she wanted Dan to stay and continue supplying her with high quality produce at preferential rates. She just stroked his arm sympathetically. Dan shared with her another reason he hated Bucket Street: Mr Shorty Johnson, the local villain. He chose not to expand on Mr Shorty Johnson to Emma, wanting her to enjoy a honeymoon period for her café.

The proprietor of the newsagent's on the other side of *Crumpets* had seen it all before. He was a tall man whose pallor gave the distinct impression he had lived his whole life in a cupboard! Signs everywhere in his shop declared that he always prosecuted thieves and asking for credit would embarrass both parties. "Them pots of flowers won't last long. They'll be on sale down the market before you know it. They'll thieve your dentures if you fall asleep around here. And them shiny windows will be good for target practice when the local hoodies come around. Shady lot they are. And you wait till you meet Shorty Johnson - or 'Mr Johnson' as he likes to be called – and his thugs, let's see how good all your fancy ideas are then," he ranted at Emma. As far as she could ascertain, he lived on his own and enquiries about his family and background were strictly taboo.

Yet not even the newsagent's grumbles and warnings could dim Emma's shine; just a couple of weeks in, *Crumpets* already felt like home.

# CHAPTER 3

Slowly but surely the reputation of *Crumpets* grew. The windows sparkled and the brass door furniture shone mirroring the welcome. The sign above the door was amusing to all the lorry drivers, each of them making the same joke as if they were the first to think of it.

Breakfast was frantic for the early starters, but more leisurely morning coffee and pastries were available for later risers. Lunch was a feast, each meal being accompanied by an obligatory bucket of chips. Afternoon tea with crumpets, scones, cream and jam became equally popular with lonely, elderly folk and exhausted young mums after the school run. For the workmen who couldn't stop, there was always coffee and accompanying bacon cobs to go. Not cobs made with a thin sliver of bacon that could be seen through, but a huge slab of the best bacon from the butcher's next door, oozing flavour and smelling mouth-wateringly good. The bacon cobs and coffee brought lorry drivers, builders and white-van-drivers to *Crumpets* from miles around.

Not only was Emma's café beginning to thrive, but so were its neighbours. First came a new blue and white striped awning outside the butcher's, followed by a lick of paint and crisp new whites. Then, amazingly, fresh paint appeared on the cynical newsagent's front door. Faded advertisements were taken down, windows cleaned, the rubbish bin emptied and the shop front swept; its first makeover for many years.

The little trio of shops became really busy, each benefitting by the increased footfall. Emma contacted the council who repaired the damaged streetlights, brightening the street no end. Even the graffiti started to fade from the area around the shops and café. The butcher's awning, some tables and chairs outside *Crumpets* and even some new ice cream adverts outside the newsagents had started to bring Bucket Street back to life. The trio of shops became an oasis of colour in the tired street.

A happy but exhausted Emma was about to close the shop one evening when she noticed three youths on the opposite side of the road. Like all youngsters they were gangly and awkward in their own skins, wearing hoodies deliberately designed to obscure their faces and giving them mysterious, intimidating appearances. They kept eyeing *Crumpets* and edging closer, furtively looking up and down the street. They clearly didn't want to give the impression that they were remotely interested, but curiosity was getting the better of them.

Emma plucked up her courage, walked across and introduced herself. Then she said something that made their eyes sparkle, "I'm just about to shut up shop and put a couple of pizzas in the oven, if you're interested? On the house."

Emma watched the three of them shuffle in front of her into the bright, airy café, looking around everywhere. She noted that they chose to sit down at a table in one of the bay windows, with their hoods still up and their hands awkwardly deep in their pockets. Emma knew that the neighbourhoods' general opinion of youngsters wearing hoodies meant trouble. The collective assumption was they would be shoplifting as soon as the proprietor's back was turned. They would undoubtably be unpleasant, loud and probably be casing the shop to come back later to burgle. They weren't welcomed in any of the other local shops and whenever they did legitimately enter, they were followed and watched by staff the whole time. Being welcomed into a new, really clean café was obviously a brand-new experience.

Emma shouted small talk from the kitchen as she prepared the pizzas with toppings that were twice as thick as usual. Finally, she brought the pizzas to the table.

"Well, you know my name, what are your names then?"

"I'm Jumbo 'cos I'm fat," replied the biggest youth peering out of his hoodie and nodding a greeting at Emma. The other two laughed at his abruptness. Jumbo continued, "That's Bean." He pointed at his mate.

Emma looked quizzically at the boy on hearing his name.

"He's got a younger bruvver who couldn't say Algernon," explained Jumbo. "Thank the lord Bean was 'appy wiv Bean or he would have had to fight everyone in school 'cos of 'is stupid name. Algernon, for goodness sake! 'Is Mum was always shouting at 'im, 'Where've you been?' So it stuck with his younger bruvver and all 'is mates cottoned on to the name. He's OK wif Bean, anyfink's better than bloody Algernon."

Bean nodded at Emma.

"And this is Mollie. She's called Mollie 'cos that's 'er name."

Mollie looked out from her hoodie and smiled a shallow smile. Her nose ring caught the light.

Emma wondered if Mollie was waiting for the inevitable judgement but no judgement would be forthcoming from her. Emma never dreamed there would be a girl in the group, but as youngsters were generally slightly built, that is, apart from Jumbo, Mollie hadn't stood out.

After the introductions, Emma duly sliced the pizzas. To the kids' evident amazement, she sat down to eat with them. She was astonished at the speed with which the pizzas were demolished. When she mentioned how fast they ate, Jumbo explained that when food was on the table in his high rise council flat, there were two types of eaters in his family: "The quick and the bloody 'ungry."

"I'm amazed you're not called Lightning then!" Emma said and they all laughed.

While Emma got up to fetch drinks, she heard Mollie whisper to Jumbo, "Stop swearing, she's being really kind to us and probably doesn't swear."

The hoodies were polite and genuine in their thanks. Emma didn't know it at the time but a couple of pizzas and a few minutes of her time would turn out to be one of the best investments she could ever have made in her early days in Bucket Street.

When her guests had gone, Emma was about to lock up and finally go up to her flat when there was an abrupt knock at the door.

Standing there was a smartly dressed short man in a camel hair coat beckoning her over. She gingerly opened the door and without being invited, he stepped inside as though he owned the place. He wore a selection of heavy bling around his neck and more jangled from his wrist. He introduced himself," My name is Mr Johnson." The name registered immediately with Emma from an earlier conversation with the newsagent and Dan.

Mr Johnson's supercilious tone explained, "You haven't been in this neighbourhood long, darling, so you won't know that it can be a very difficult place in which to trade if you didn't know the right people." He sniffed as he walked about the café valuing everything as he went. "There are ruffians and thieves everywhere, but the worst of the lot are the hoodies. Nasty kids are the hoodies." Without waiting for a comment from Emma he went on to say, "Windows get smashed and all manner of dreadful things happen here. All the shops needed insurance." He was about to help himself to a piece of cake from the cake plate under its glass dome when Emma moved it further along the counter out of reach. He continued, "Well, it's your lucky day, darling, for I am able to offer that very insurance. For a small sum each week you would be able to sleep easy in your bed knowing that your café is safe in my hands."

Despite the after-hours intrusion and the man's haughty manner, Emma kept her cool and asked, "And just how much is this protection?"

"Not protection, please." Mr Johnson tutted and shook his head. He continued, "It's insurance. £100 per week and you'll be pleased to note that there's no VAT on top of that." He chortled.

"£100 per week?" exclaimed Emma. "£100?" she repeated, doing the sums in her head. "That's more than I currently take. It's impossible. I can't pay that."

"Then you'll just have to work harder, work longer, put your prices up or pay your yourself less. Now, I'm not an unreasonable man and I've let you have a few weeks free while you settled in, so let's call it £50 for this week and £100 a week from now on." He turned to the door and added, "Oh, I nearly forgot, two of my lads will be round on Friday evening to collect the money. Good night, darling." Before he left, he looked her up and down leering at her shape and left the door wide open as he stepped out onto the pavement.

# CHAPTER 4

The following week, Emma worried constantly about the forthcoming visit by Mr Johnson's thugs. She could neither eat nor concentrate. She ordered enough tea for three months by mistake and slept completely through the alarm one morning. She also gave one customer change for a £10 note instead of £5, which thankfully he pointed out to her.

Over coffee with Dan during one of her quiet times, she asked him what he did about Mr Johnson.

Dan shrugged his shoulders and said resignedly, "What options have I got? Dad paid it and I pay it. Every Friday they come around and I hand over £100. That's how it is, and will always be. It's just over £5,000 each year off the bottom line. Dad used to make me stay behind to pay it, saying he could well do something stupid with a meat cleaver if he was there. Every Friday now I wish he had."

"Well, I'm not paying it!" declared Emma, grimacing at the thought of handing over anything to the slimy man. How am I supposed to pay the mortgage? How am I supposed to pay the electric bill and the water rates? How am I supposed to buy stock, cooking oils, bread, milk, your bacon or eggs while he sits on his bum and gets fat?"

Dan shook his head as a warning.

The next day Emma talked to the newsagent who just raised his eyebrows and said much the same. However, he added a further note of caution that if she took on Shorty Johnson, they would all suffer. Emma stomped out of his shop.

That evening she raised the subject with the hoodies, who had quickly become regular customers of *Crumpets*. They were not keen to talk about Shorty Johnson at first, but when she explained how he had intimidated her they opened up.

Bean answered on behalf of them all, "Shorty Johnson is the self-styled, local Mafia and he's been around all our lives. He's a small-time crook who runs a protection racket in the neighbourhood." Jumbo and Mollie nodded.

Mollie added, "We've heard bits and rumours about what he's supposed to have had done to folk who took him on in the past. He's probably lived on the stories for years but we've never seen any evidence of him hurting anyone."

Jumbo between mouthfuls of pizza said, "We've 'eard 'e systematically squeezed all the shopkeepers out of the area. 'Es plain greedy; 'ad 'e asked for just a little amount then most would 'ave paid up and not turned a 'air. Instead, 'e made them pay so 'eavily that they was working for nufink. 'e must 'ave been absolutely delighted to see you and your café opening up on 'is manor,"

Emma's worrying built up as the end of the week approached. She was a nervous wreck as she locked up on Friday evening. Then she heard a big car draw up outside

*Crumpets* followed by several very loud unsettling knocks at the door, she dutifully went and let the two thugs in. They were middle-aged, overweight men wearing ill-fitting, shabby suits. Both had shaved heads and the smaller of the two had blurred tattoos across the back of both of his hands. There was no mistaking they were definitely Shorty's thugs.

Emma noticed the hoodies watching from the other aside of the street. She hoped they wouldn't get involved.

The bigger of the two men said, "We've come for the Friday collection."

"Just exactly what do I get for my money?" snapped Emma bravely, standing with her hands on her hips, stalling before parting with the hard-earned, inevitable payment.

"Well now, Darlin', you get complete protection from every villain who operates around these parts," said the bigger thug.

Just then there was a crash of glass outside the shop. They all looked at the door, but when nothing or nobody immediately materialised, the thugs turned back to Emma. However, a second crash soon followed, even louder than the first, from the direction of their shiny, black BMW car.

The smaller thug casually went to the window to investigate what was happening in the street, then shouted back to his mate, "Some b****** has just smashed both our headlights and there's glass all over the road". As he shouted, there were two more crashes and the glass of both rear lights fell out onto the road.

Both thugs rushed out of the shop, looking for the culprits. They eventually drove off, hanging out of the windows while searching the area for the miscreants, and shouting what they would do if they caught them.

Still, Emma was in tears over her visit from the thugs. They had invaded her space. It wasn't fair. She was about to lock up for second time when there was a tapping at the window. The three hoodies peered in.

She composed herself first, then let them in. After retrieving three Cokes from the fridge, she warmed some scones and sat down with them. They needed to have a serious talk.

"Now listen, you guys, I know you want to help, but I want you to stay out of this business with Shorty Johnson. Do you understand?" Her voice wasn't hostile or parental, it was a voice full of concern for them. These youngsters had become her friends and she didn't want them hurt.

Jumbo was the first to speak and said flatly, "We didn't do nufink." He pushed his hands deep into his pockets and looked at his feet.

Emma realised they were hardly likely to admit smashing car headlights and rear lights. "It's really sweet of you and I know you won't admit anything, but please let me handle it. OK?" she said, ending the conversation.

They nodded in unison, shrugging their shoulders in a, 'whatever' pose.

It was Mollie who eventually said, "You were going to hand over the cash, weren't you?"

Emma had to admit she was.

# CHAPTER 5

The next Friday came around and Emma spent the whole day unable to take her eyes off the front door. She shook at the slightest sound, waiting for the dreaded knock.

It came at exactly the same time as the previous week. It was going dark, not many people about and she had just cashed up. Emma let the thugs in with no greeting.

The bigger of the two spoke first. "We've come for the money – this week's and last week's. That's £150 in total, darlin'. You don't have to add a tip for good service, but all contributions are gratefully received! Eh, 'Arry?"

The other thug – Harry – replied with a smirk, "Yerr, always, yerr right, 'Enry."

Emma couldn't help but have a cheeky jibe. "You're a good protection firm, can't even keep your own car safe. What was it – two smashed headlights and two smashed taillights right outside my café with both of you in here not ten feet away? How do you intend to keep my café and all its contents safe? Is this good value for money?"

Her cross side was peeping through. Her 'this is unfair side' was showing and she knew they could both see fire in her eyes.

"Where've you parked your car today then?" she mocked. "Or did you come by bus?" She wondered if she had overstepped the mark with the bus jibe.

"It's around the corner under a street lamp where Mr Johnson told us to put it. Nobody'll touch it there. Me and 'Arry'll catch the hoodies what did it last week and when we do, they'll be real sorry. Isn't that so, 'Arry?"

"Yerr," replied a disinterested Harry who was looking out of the window more concerned by the noise that was going on outside. He could hear the shrill siren of an ambulance or a police car a street or two away, getting louder by the second. Sirens, particularly police sirens, held a special dread for him making him very jittery. He paced about, not going anywhere in particular, repeatedly glancing back at the shop windows. Suddenly, the blue flashing lights of a fire engine lit up the café as it sped past, then another and another.

The bigger thug stopped to watch the spectacle through the windows.

When the lights of the tenders had passed, Harry eventually came out from behind the curtains now a shade braver.

"I expect it's one of those folks what don't have any insurance, eh, 'Enry?" They both laughed nervously.

Just then, Dan from next door popped his head in to say there was a big fire burning around the corner – a brand-new, white, BMW was on fire.

The two thugs looked at each other and groaned.

"Oh f***!" they said in unison and sped out of the shop, pushing past the butcher.

"Something I said?" enquired Dan playfully as he watched the two men race off down the street.

Emma breathed a huge sigh of relief but inside was struggling to hold back the tears.

"Are you OK, Emma? Can I get you something?" he asked, very concerned and not prepared to take that she was OK for an answer. He led her to a table in the window, pulled a chair up for her and sat her down. Without asking, he went behind the counter and made her a hot chocolate drink. He sat with her until he could see the colour returning to her face.

"I'm OK now," she assured him. "Thank you, Dan."

He appeared reluctant to leave but stopped at the door and said, "You know you can just call me if you feel frightened again. I'm just next door. I'll come straight away."

Emma waited for the tap on the window that came shortly after Dan had gone. In came the three hoodies.

"Shame that, eh? Nice White BMW. Looked new to me," commented Jumbo. Yer, three fire engines it took to put it out. Wonder whose it could've been. Nobody round 'ere 'as one of them posh motors," Jumbo was taking off his hoodie as if at home. "It didn't 'arf go up, Emma, explosions and sparks and all sorts, just like firework night." He waved his arms to emphasise the size of them and made noises of the explosions.

Emma just listened as she set up the Cokes and pizzas. Mollie was quiet and helped her. Bean and Jumbo sat in the window seats recounting the incident as though the other had not been there. When they were all sat around the table and had a big piece of pizza in their mouths, Emma took the opportunity to speak.

"Now listen, you guys, I need to talk to you again. This is getting really nasty. Shorty's men don't mess about. They already think it was some hoodies who damaged their first car. It won't take them long to hear about you three coming in here regularly, put two and two together and come looking for you. I really don't want that." Emma continued, "You're a super bunch of kids and I don't expect you to own up to anything. Goodness only knows how many things you've been blamed for that you didn't do. Please, please don't get involved in this."

Jumbo snapped a reply, "Right, Emma, listen carefully. We told you last time and we'll tell you again – we don't know nufink about it, OK?" He nodded in a 'this conversation is finished' way.

"He's right, Em, we don't know nufink," reaffirmed Mollie quietly. "We were someplace else when it went up."

Emma looked at them doubtfully, but they all shrugged.

"Whatever," they said in unison.

———

Two days after the excitement with the fire engines, Emma was sweeping through the café at closing time when the bell jangled a warning. Harry the thug roughly pushed open the door and the three hoodies tumbled into the café and sprawled across the floor.

Jumbo protested his innocence as he landed, scattering the tables and chairs, "We din't do nufink!"

Henry shut the door and locked it. Emma began to think this was about to turn really violent with her and the three kids getting hurt. Is this the end of *Crumpets?* flashed through her mind. This had all the makings of not ending well.

"Let the kids go," she pleaded. "I'll pay you all the money. Just let them go." As she was pleading, Emma slid along the inside of the counter to get out into the main café main area and then try to get between the thugs and the hoodies.

As she did, Henry deliberately nudged the three-tier glass cake stand off the counter and Emma watched helplessly as it smashed into a thousand pieces on the floor, spilling Victoria sponge slices, muffins and glass everywhere. It was the centre piece of the counter and her pride and joy. It was the first thing she had bought for the café out of her profits. Her hands went to her open mouth and tears streamed down her face.

"Oh dear, oh dear, I do 'ope you're insured," said the bigger thug, laughing.

Mollie was first on her feet. She swore at him as she went to push him away from the counter. She was beside herself in a complete temper, shouting at him to leave Emma alone. His hand moved quickly and he hit her hard on the side of her head. She landed, in a crumpled heap, about six feet away.

Jumbo and Bean immediately went to help her, but Henry shouted, "Stay where you are or you'll get a taste of the same!" He gestured as though he was going to hit Jumbo too. The boy backed away, terrified. "And you stay exactly where you are too, lady, you're not too old to get one too."

Jumbo and Bean froze; everything was happening very fast. Mollie lay still on the floor, unconscious.

Emma was in shock, tears still running down her cheeks. She couldn't move a muscle, not even to go to Mollie.

Just as Henry started walking away from the kids to join his mate at the counter, a circular, metal tea tray mysteriously flew into the air from the dirty pots trolley. It travelled the ten feet, gathering speed all the way, and hit him squarely in his pock-marked face. He didn't see it coming until it was too late. Bang!

Solid as he was, his legs flew forward, his head snapped back and he landed heavily on his backside. He just sat there, his glazed-over eyes rolling around and around in his head. Suddenly, his body went limp and his head slumped backwards, banging on the floor with a sickening thud. Blood ran out of both nostrils across his cheeks. Henry was out cold.

As soon as it was certain that he wasn't going to get back up, the hovering metal tea tray with the imprint of the thug's forehead and new nose, silently returned to its original place on the dirty pots station.

Mollie was just beginning to stir, but Emma, Jumbo and Bean, who had seen everything, were speechless.

The only person who'd had his back to the incident was Harry. He hadn't seen a thing. He'd been too busy concentrating on intimidating the tearful Emma and preventing her from going to Mollie. He thought that the commotion was coming from his mate Henry knocking the kids around a bit.

Emma, Jumbo and Bean kept looking, first at Henry unconscious on the floor and then at the deformed metal tea tray.

Harry, still completely unaware of what had just happened behind him, had spread some bogus insurance papers out on the counter. He held a short, stubby pencil, about three inches long, between the tips of each of his index fingers. He gestured for Emma to sign the papers.

"The pencil's a bit blunt. You can sharpen it if you want, but it won't make a scrap of difference. You can even mark it with a cross if you like." He laughed at his own weird humour.

As he ogled and gestured menacingly at Emma, an ornamental meat cleaver silently removed itself from the wall display above the counter and with a swift slice chopped the stubby pencil in two. Each half spun into the air. The meat cleaver travelled onwards through all the papers, ending its journey stuck upright and embedded deep into the polished counter.

Harry checked his index fingers were still attached, gulped and slowly stepped backwards, not taking his eyes off the meat cleaver. All the blood in his face quickly drained away.

Everyone was silent.

Emma gaped, her gaze bouncing between Harry and then the meat cleaver. The two hoodies, who hadn't seen what happened at the counter looked back and forwards at the dented metal tea tray and the still unconscious bigger thug.

The silence in the café was shattered by the sound of broken glass outside. Everyone looked towards the third, damaged, BMW car parked out in the street. Then there was another crash.

Harry groaned. "Not again," he said as the second headlight flew in diamond shapes all over the road.

Jumbo jumped up and shouted at Harry, "There! You wouldn't listen, would yer? I told you we didn't do nufink. We woz bloody-well in 'ere wif you, wasn't we? All of us, wasn't we? It couldn't be us, see. Nobody ever listens. It's always the bloody same, nobody believes us. We didn't do nufink to your crappy old cars."

Harry kicked Henry to wake him but to no avail; he was in a different world. Lifting a jug of flowers off one of the nearby tables he sloshed the water inside, including the flowers, into the prostrate man's face. He woke, spluttering and coughing, to the musical sound of the rear lights on the BMW being smashed, first on one side then the other.

The two of them angrily fumbled to get the door open, barging each other before running out into the street in search of whoever had damaged the third BMW in three weeks.

Then Henry jumped into the light-less car and drove off. Loose wires trailed out of each light's mounting and noisy red reflectors bounced along the road giving the impression of a wedding car. Harry ran down the side alleyways.

Shorty is not going to be a happy bunny tonight, thought Emma.

They all helped Mollie to her feet and the four of them looked at each other in complete disbelief.

"Don't ask me. I don't know either," Emma pre-empted their questions.

She walked over to the pile of tea trays and examined the top one. She ran her fingers over the new profile. It was dented beyond recognition. Remembering where it had been, she replaced it quickly.

Bean was really struggling to release the ornamental meat cleaver from the counter and Jumbo was looking down at the remains of the cake stand.

He absently said, "I really liked that cake stand. Why would anyone do that to it? What possible pleasure could 'e 'ave got from doing that? I'll clear it up."

"Thank you, Jumbo, but just leave it. I'll do it in the morning. I can't face doing it now." Emma sighed.

"We'll help," said Bean as he held the dented metal tea tray up to his face to see if the profile fitted.

"Gosh 'e 'ad a big nose," said Jumbo.

"Not anymore," said Bean and all four of them laughed.

Mollie, who had just about recovered from her ordeal, was having a turn at trying to pull the meat cleaver out of the counter, but it wouldn't budge. Emma explained, as best she could, what had happened while Mollie had still been coming round.

Mollie muttered, "I wish it 'ad been 'is 'ed." She winced as she touched her bruised eye.

"You're all very kind offering to help, but it's getting late and you need to be home, not out in the streets with those two thugs looking for someone to take it out on."

"You're right," said Mollie, "It's later than I thought. My Mum'll be worrying. I'll come back as early as I can get away tomorrow, Emma to help clean up."

"Me too," chorused the other two.

Emma hugged the three of them and reinforced her warning. "You know you guys have had a narrow escape from those two thugs tonight, don't you? Now promise me not a word to anyone. Not one word. If those two or Shorty Johnson think people are laughing at them, then heaven only knows what they're capable of. Now, each of you, promise me."

In turn they promised.

Emma ushered them out, repeating again that they must not say a word to anyone.

"And take extra care on the way home please," she said.

The three of them slipped out into the familiar shadows of the back-streets and headed for home.

When Emma was sure that the café was safely locked with a chain on the front and back doors, she made herself a mug of hot chocolate and sat in the comfy winged chair by the window to think. The meat cleaver was still stuck in the counter as a reminder that this had not been a dream and the deformed metal tea tray was back on the dirty pots station. This has been a real live incident that could have turned very unpleasant, if whatever happened had not happened, she thought to herself.

Emma considered ringing the police but Shorty Johnson's words kept coming back to her: "Most of the local plod work for me anyway."

# CHAPTER 6

Emma woke with the mug of hot chocolate precariously balanced in her hands. She had fallen fast asleep, a delayed reaction to the ordeal. Her foggy brain wasn't functioning, she didn't know how long she had been asleep, and she was being gently woken by a smart gentleman who was taking her hot drink out of her hands to prevent it from spilling. He wasn't frightening but Emma didn't recognise him, nor could she understand how he had got in.

She looked at the locked front door then back to the gentleman. She was about to get up when he introduced himself most courteously.

"Good evening, Emma, please don't be alarmed. My name's Arthur, Arthur Densill, please don't get up." Then he turned to a lady who was standing close behind him, who Emma hadn't been able to see at first. He stepped aside and introduced her. "This is Martha, Mrs Martha Dunkton-Jones." She gave a friendly wave of her gloved hand and smiled. "You've had a very nasty experience here tonight, my dear," Arthur went on to say. "We're really pleased we were nearby and able to help. However, I must humbly apologise about the damage done to your beautifully polished counter by the meat cleaver, but it was the only thing I could think of on the spur of the moment. It did work famously though, didn't it?" Arthur chuckled. "I liked the bit when the thug shook his fingers to make sure they were all still attached. I'll see if there's something I can do about the counter top later."

Emma was speechless. For the second time that evening she did not know what to say. She kept looking at this kindly old gentleman and elegant lady then back at the locked door.

"Where... where have you come from?" she stuttered when she found her voice again. "Did you come in through the back door? I could have sworn I'd locked it and it's got a safety chain on." She pointed at the meat cleaver and looked at Arthur. "That was you?" Not waiting for an answer, she said, "Please don't think I'm ungrateful in any way. On the contrary, I'm really grateful. I think you probably saved my café and me, not to mention Mollie, Bean and Jumbo. Just tell me... where have you come from, Mrs Dunkton-Jones?"

"Oh, we live here," said Martha, matter of factly, as she plumped up a cushion on a nearby chair and sat down. "And please call me Martha."

"You live where?" asked a confused Emma, shaking her head.

"Here at number 52 Bucket Street," stated Martha. "With you."

"I'm sorry?" Emma questioned. She leaned forward. "Just run that by me again, please."

"Yes, my dear," replied Martha. "Please just relax and we'll explain. Arthur, pull up another chair and sit down."

Arthur dutifully did as he was told and Emma relaxed back into her winged chair. Arthur passed her back the mug of chocolate now her hands were steady and Emma took a large swallow. The sugar hit activated almost immediately, helping to clear her pea soup head.

"Arthur and I have lived here for years. Yes, years and years. Haven't we, Arthur?" Martha was smoothing his jacket sleeve affectionately as she looked for confirmation from him.

Arthur nodded his agreement and smiled warmly back at her. He passed his hand over hers and patted it.

Emma looked back and forth between them then over to the meat cleaver and smashed cake stand. The whole unsavoury evening came flooding back and she started to cry and shake, spilling her hot chocolate. Arthur gently eased the mug from Emma's hand again and placed it on a nearby table.

"Don't worry. You're safe, my dear. Nobody's going to harm you now," said Arthur.

Emma found her handkerchief, wiped her eyes, blew her nose and stood up, trying to compose herself. "Right, now please help me to get this straight. You two firstly bent one of my metal tea trays beyond recognition around the face of one thug and then frightened the other out of his mind with a meat cleaver. "Am I right so far?"

"Well, yes." Arthur nodded. "I suppose so."

"Then you went outside and smashed both the headlights on their latest BMW. Is that right?"

"Don't forget the tail lights too. We've had such fun tonight, haven't we, Arthur?" chipped in Martha.

"We certainly have, Martha. I can't think when we last enjoyed ourselves more. Setting the white BMW on fire was certainly the biggest display of our work, but the hand-to-hand stuff of tonight will definitely top the bill for me." Arthur smiled to himself at the memories of the evening and held up an imaginary tray, demonstrating how he bent it beyond recognition. "Although we really didn't mean to torch the white BMW car, more to... what's the phrase? Just do the tyres. I suppose we got a little carried away, but you do in the heat of the moment when you're having fun, don't you, my dear? No pun intended." She chuckled at her own joke about the heat of the moment.

"Did you also smash in the headlights of the thugs' first black car. Was that you too?"

"I'm afraid so," replied Martha, raising her shoulders mischievously.

Emma twigged for the first time that the hoodies had been telling the truth all the time. She felt awful that she hadn't believed them about smashing the lights and torching the car. She remembered Jumbo proclaiming their innocence while they were in the café at the same time as the thugs. She felt so bad. Next time she saw them she would have to thoroughly apologise.

Emma walked around the tables, her shoes crunching the broken glass.

"Have you any idea who those people were?" asked Emma, her hands emphasising her concern. "And what they are capable of? They're really evil and will do anything their boss tells them to do."

"Yes, my dear, we are well aware of who they are. They are the henchmen of Shorty Johnson. I remember his father; he was a nasty piece of work too. Finished his days in the scrubs if I'm not mistaken," said Martha. "However, don't you worry, we're here now. They're just bullies, aren't they, Arthur? Don't you fret, my dear, I doubt they'll be back, but if they do come, we'll be waiting for them."

Emma didn't understand anything about what was happening. She shook her head to try to wake herself up from the dream she was sure she was trapped in and decided to start again.

"I'm sorry to sound a bit slow, but please tell me again where you said you lived?"

Emma looked around her café expecting to see a couple of bunk beds in the corner with a nightie draped on one and some striped pyjamas on the other. Something, anything, to confirm what had she had just been told. She didn't know whether to run out of the café screaming, frightened witless, or just be so grateful for their intervention. But they weren't scary or alarming; more like an old aunt and uncle.

Arthur patiently began, "I know it sounds a bit strange, but we both live here with you, my dear. Let me explain. Long, long ago this place used to be a family undertakers. About fifty years ago. And, I have to say, it was a very good undertakers whose reputation in the community was second to none. Well, when it was my turn to go, and it comes to us all at some time or other, my dead body was brought here. My wife made all the funeral arrangements with the proprietor and, even though I do say it myself, she organised a very good send off for me. There were bottles and bottles of very good quality Amontillado sherry and ham off the bone in the sandwiches. There were vol-au-vents, delicate cheese straws and fresh salmon slices in thinly cut brown bread triangles, without crusts! None of your basic corned beef sandwiches or cubes of cheddar cheese impaled on tooth picks stuck into a tin foil wrapped potato. There were no pickled onions or cheap beer that some folks had either. I couldn't have been more proud of her."

Arthur waited while Emma caught up with him, before continuing, "My coffin was real English oak, not pine or orange box wood, like some of the cheapskates around here would have had, but really good quality, solid English oak; a fine piece of workmanship. I was really impressed. I was laid out on that very same counter top that you so lovingly restored and polished."

Emma's mouth was wide open and she immediately snatched her hand off the counter top as a mark of respect to all those who had used it as their departure lounge.

During Arthur's explanation, Emma studied his and Martha's appearances. They were both dressed smartly, in the sort of clothes her grandparents used to wear when they were having visitors or going to chapel.

Arthur wore a double-breasted dark suit and a mustard-coloured waistcoat complete with watch and chain. He sported a short goatee beard and had silver hair with the odd flicked-up curl at the back. A perfectly tied Windsor tie and pair of brightly polished brown shoes suggested a possible military background.

Martha wore a long, cream, elegant, lace dress, which didn't quite reach to the floor. A tasteful jabot was pinned into the neck of the dress. A pashmina stole, the same colour as her dress, was draped over her shoulders and her white hair was tightly coiffured. Embroidered cream gloves complemented her outfit.

Martha couldn't wait for Arthur to continue their story so impatiently jumped in, "Now, you won't know this yet, my dear, but once you are in the coffin you get a visit from a man called 'the transporter'. He's a kindly old man who arranges everything for you. He transports you to Heaven in your real travel coffin. It's a metallic version, like a bob sleigh. Before you go, he arranges a replica of you to be left here on Earth for those who are left behind to do with whatever they want. Sometimes they bury your replica and sometimes they cremate it. Nobody can tell the difference from the real thing and everybody's happy."

Martha was in full swing so Emma decided not to interrupt. She was enraptured.

"Well," she continued, "just before you are 'transported' you are also offered the opportunity to go back and visit a loved one, only if you want to that is. Just for a short time. You are allowed to return and say your goodbyes. Of course, they can't see or hear you properly, but it makes you feel better, especially if you weren't together when you died. Well, I really wanted to see my husband of forty-nine years again. I was out shopping when I was called and didn't see him again. We parted in the morning after having a bit of a tiff about something silly. I just couldn't go and not say I was sorry. I loved him so much."

Emma nodded, eager to hear more.

"Well, I popped back to see him and found him so full of remorse having parted with me in a grump that I just couldn't leave him. You must have heard people say that after they have lost someone special, they sometimes see them standing at the foot of the bed. Or they feel a breath of air on their cheek when whoever has died leans forward to give them a last kiss. Well, I just couldn't leave him, I just couldn't and stayed all night. When I returned here to the funeral parlour, I was too late. My heavenly coffin had gone without me. My replica and my coffin had gone to be cremated." Martha sighed gently and gave Emma a small smile.

"So, you see, my dear, I was left behind, as was Arthur when he visited his wife for the last time. I was so pleased I wasn't left here alone. I don't know what I would have done without him, he's been such a dear." Martha gave Arthur a little squeeze on the arm and then wiped a tear from her cheek.

"Where do you sleep?" asked the incredulous Emma. "What exactly do you do all day long?"

"Well, we don't need to sleep like we used to, so during the daytime we split up and go off to visit other folk who have been left behind and we return when you're asleep. We sit in your armchairs and chat about the day. I must say you have made such a lovely job of the café. Sometimes we finish clearing up when you're so tired you just go to bed. I hope that's all right; we didn't think you'd mind."

There had been nights when Emma could hardly put one foot in front of the other. She had been so exhausted she just abandoned the kitchen till the morning. Yet the next day, everywhere was always neat and tidy. She concluded she must have forgotten she had finished cleaning up, such was her tiredness.

"When you first came to view the place," continued Martha, "we really didn't want to be disturbed. We nearly didn't let you in."

"Yes, we both pushed and pushed against the door when you tried to get in with your young man," jumped in Arthur.

"He was very strong. However, it's been so exciting here at *Crumpets* over the last few months we are really pleased you did get in."

"How will you get back?" asked Emma becoming drawn into this strange, strange world.

"There's only one way to get the transporter back here, and that is to be in a coffin in the same place as we were last time he came. He believes he missed us and makes all the arrangements. Well, that's never going to happen because we don't have our coffins – they have been burned or buried. So here we are, and homeless. We'd love to stay, if you'll have us? We promise not to get in the way."

"I think that's a decision for another day," suggested Arthur tactfully.

# CHAPTER 7

Emma slept fitfully that night, unsure as to what was happening in her life. She had upset the local Mafia and put two fingers up to their protection racket. However, *Crumpets* was doing very well, the local hoodies were her friends and now there were two delightful spooks living downstairs. It was all barmy.

After an hour of tossing and turning, she popped down to see if Arthur and Martha were still there. She found them sitting in her armchairs chatting and they both gave her a smile and a little wave goodnight. Without saying anything, Emma waved back nervously and retired to bed.

She woke again early and went down in her dressing gown to make a cup of tea. The meat cleaver was hanging up back on the wall and the damage to the counter had been repaired, just as Arthur had promised. All that remained was a tiny mark. The smashed cake stand and all the glass had been cleared away.

As the memory of the previous evening came flooding back it made her shudder and challenge her sanity. There was a familiar tap at the window she immediately recognised as that of the hoodies. Unusually, Mollie was on her own and sporting a huge bruise on her cheek and a black eye.

"You OK. Mollie?" asked an anxious Emma looking at her face.

"Yes fine. Face is a bit colourful but I'm fine, is everything all right with you Em? The thugs didn't come back, did they?" she asked.

Emma gave her a hug for her kindness and promptly burst into tears. Mollie seemed to sense exactly what she needed and held her tightly for a few moments. Emma then sat down and Mollie made them some tea.

Emma relayed what a dreadful night's sleep she'd had following the visit from the thugs. "I've got to tell someone what else happened last night as if the thugs weren't enough. I fell asleep in the chair in the window and when I woke there were two people in the café. I have never seen before but they weren't intimidating. They said they lived here in 52, Bucket Street and had done for years and years and they were the ones who sorted the thugs out with the tray and the meat cleaver."

Mollie listened with one eye as open as it could be. She then said, "But we didn't see anyone else in the café. Where had they come from?"

"Well, apparently they are spirits who are caught in the between worlds."

"And I thought it was just me that had the bang on the head!" Mollie chipped in.

She couldn't get her head around the explanation either and in the absence of logic they laughed at the ridiculousness of it all. However, evidence was still there in the form of the dented metal tea tray and the mark in the counter left by the meat cleaver.

Emma was relieved to be able to share how she felt with Mollie. Nothing made any sense, but talking helped her.

Mollie knew that in the absence of reason, tea was always a good distraction and started to make another pot just for the two of them, this time with some buttered hot toast.

While they ate the toast they chatted about life in general when Mollie suggested things were beginning to pile up on Emma and perhaps she wasn't thinking too clearly.

"You're right. Let's sort out the problems one by one," said Emma, trying to be logical. "First, what shall I do about the local Mafia?"

There was a long silence. Both shrugged their shoulders.

"OK, next, how do I help my two spooks? They are delightful and I actually quite like them, but I get the impression they both really want to leave this Earthly place and go wherever they should have gone."

Mollie then said, quite matter-of-factly, "Well, it sounds as if all you need are a couple of coffins for a night."

"Oh, and where do you suggest I get a couple of coffins, may I ask? A car boot sale? I can honestly say I didn't see one coffin for sale at the last car boot sale I went to, not one! Or how about an ad in the wanted column of the local rag: 'Two coffins required for one night only. One large, one small, to be returned the next day'?"

"Don't be sarky, Emma, I'm really trying to help," admonished Mollie.

"Sorry," replied the contrite Emma. "How do you think you can help then?"

"We borrow a couple of coffins. Bean has a mate. The miserable looking sod was snatched up to work in an undertaker's on the other side of town as soon as he was old enough to leave school and he still works there now. Looks just as miserable as he did then. Bean'll ask him, I'm sure. Come on, you only want to borrow them for a night so nothing's going to happen to them, is it? What can possibly go wrong?"

"I hate it when folk say that," said Emma.

"The real owners won't complain, will they? I'll ask Bean later today, OK?"

"Well, when you put it like that, I don't see the harm in it at all." Emma shook her head in complete disbelief before giving Mollie a big thank you hug. "I can't start to tell you, Bean or Jumbo how sorry I am for doubting you over the smashed lamps on the BMWs."

Mollie gave her a 'we've been here before look' and was gone.

———

The day ended normally enough. Emma had been run off her feet and when she turned around it was past 6.00 p.m. The one thing she had promised herself all day long was that as soon as the day was over, she would write a card and display it in the front window: POT WASHER WANTED, GOOD PAY. It was one of the jobs she hated most. Her Marigolds were on and off all day long and the later in the day she washed up, the more often she forgot to wear them.

Her hands were now red and sore. She put the card in the bottom corner of the café's front window, crossed her fingers and hoped.

Emma wearily locked the café and started to sweep through ready for tomorrow's onslaught when she heard the wheels of a large car slow down and stop outside.

"Oh no," she groaned to herself, hiding her face in her hands and sinking into an armchair out of sight. She couldn't face another night being visited by the thugs. Now she needed Arthur and Martha more than ever. Where the hell were they? She was tired and not in the mood for a fight with – what would definitely be – two very hacked off thugs. She curled up in the winged chair like a little girl, her knees up to her chest.

There were several bangs on the door. Emma froze; perhaps they would just go away if they thought there was no one in. Thugs don't just go away, she told herself. She waited for the door to come crashing in when she heard a familiar voice from outside: "Come on, Emma, this is bloody heavy."

She quickly opened the door and was met by Mollie as well as Bean and Jumbo behind her, who were holding a coffin. And to be fair about how Mollie had described him, the most soulful, miserable looking lad in the world accompanied them. What she'd forgotten to mention was that he was about six feet six inches tall and probably by trying not to stand out from the other kids, had developed a stoop. A real funereal, reverent stoop. Emma could imagine him walking slowly in front of a cortege, dressed all in black with his head bowed.

Huffing and puffing, Bean and Jumbo brought their coffin inside while Mollie cleared the counter. Outside, the soulful lad began to unload the second coffin from the back of the hearse. Emma watched the delivery in silence, shaking her head in disbelief. After depositing their coffin, Bean and Jumbo immediately went out to help with the other.

When both coffins were finally inside the café, the soulful lad mumbled, "I don't know what you needs 'em for, so it better not be nufink dodgy, Bean. And I don't want 'em back wif 'oles in 'em where folk 'ave stuck oak stakes fru 'em, right. And listen, Bean, remember, the coffins 'as to be back in the funeral parlour real early tomorrow. Real early, got it?"

"Why the rush?" queried Bean, who knew it would be difficult to get out of his house the next morning really early, without creating suspicion.

"'Cos I just left the occupants sitting up in big chairs in the boss's office, round 'is table, that's bloody why! The parlour's full of stiffs what with the flu an' all that. I got no other place to put 'em. He'll go bonkers if he gets in before me an' sees 'em just sat there like they're playing whist. Tomorrow's cleaner's day too. They'll run out screaming blue murder if they goes into the boss's office with mops and buckets an' finds 'em first. You couldn't have picked a worse night to borrow 'em. I'll be 'ere at 6.00 am tomorrow sharp an' I'll get the sack if I'm late."

"What, the bodies are just sitting in chairs in your boss's office?" asked the incredulous Emma. "Won't they fall over or something?"

"Naa, they're stiff as broomsticks, they'll be right. Probably 'ave to jump up and down on 'em a bit to get 'em back in the coffins tomorrow," replied the lad nonchalantly as he left the café.

Emma's mouth was open wide as the ancient hearse spirited away silently in the dark night.

"There, I told you he would do it, Emma, and be happy 'bout it," said Mollie, smiling triumphantly.

"I'm not sure I'd describe him as 'happy'. Is he even old enough to drive yet?" asked a naïve Emma.

"Nearly," said Bean. "One more year and he'll be legal."

Emma just shook her head, not wanting to hear any more.

They positioned the heavy coffins end to end on the long counter with the lids off ready.

"What now?" asked Bean.

"I suppose we just wait till Arthur and Martha turn up," said Emma.

The three hoodies looked at each other apprehensively. Mollie had recounted Emma's meeting with the spooks and Bean and Jumbo had laughed nervously.

"You don't really believe all that oojey-boojey stuff, do you, Emma?" asked Jumbo. "'Cos we woz wundering if you might 'ave been 'aving a few sneaky swigs of the cooking sherry."

"Or perhaps you've bin cookin' magic mushrooms by mistake," chipped in Bean dryly, which made them all laugh.

As soon as the pizzas were placed in the oven, the group started to make up a new spooky menu for *Crumpets*, starting with Mollie's suggestion: "How about bacon and scrambled eggs on ghost?"

Then it was Jumbo's turn, "Or coffin and biscuits? Or ghoulash?"

Bean added, "Or chicken pastaway or spooketti?"

"What about dead and butter pudding? Or smashed avacadarver?" Emma shouted her offerings from the kitchen.

They all howled with laughter at each other's suggestions.

Soon piping hot pizzas were on the table and there was a delightful party atmosphere in the café, despite there being two open coffins on the counter.

Suddenly, a slice of pizza flew off the central plate in one direction and then another rose in the air and disappeared abruptly. In silence, as one, the three hoodies stood up, knocking their chairs over. They quickly backed away from the table until they were all against the far wall of the café.

Only Jumbo spoke, "What the f***"

They started to edge towards the door, not taking their eyes off the table.

Arthur and Martha suddenly materialised, waved politely to the hoodies, said hello, picked up the fallen chairs, pulled up two new chairs, sat down and reached for two more slices of pizza.

"We never had pizzas in our day, did we, Arthur? They really are spiffing, aren't they?" commented Martha.

Using a knife and fork on a plate to cut up his pizza, Arthur nodded enthusiastically. "Splendid, absolutely splendid and so kind of you to organise the coffins for us, so kind."

Shaking her head Martha said, "I just can't imagine where you could have acquired two coffins and the right sizes too. We promise we will both take great care of them. It really is so kind of you."

Slowly food began to trump fear and the hoodies moved cautiously back towards the table. It wasn't long before everyone was chatting and laughing about Shorty Johnson's thugs, life in Bucket Street in years gone by and *Crumpets's* new menu.

"Loved your 'coffin and biscuits', Jumbo," said Arthur.

"Oh, I liked Bean's 'spooketti' best," said Martha.

Eventually, the plates were empty, all the Coke had been drunk and it was time for Arthur and Martha to prepare to leave.

Lots of 'thank-yous' for the use of the coffins and 'so pleased to have met yous' followed. Both Arthur and Martha hugged Emma and wished her well with the café. The hoodies declined the hugs but did tentatively shake hands, each anxiously checking to see if any gooey ectoplasm had been left on their fingers.

Arthur was the first to climb into his coffin. He fitted perfectly. He folded his arms across his chest and closed his eyes. Martha needed a bit of a leg up by Bean and Jumbo, but eventually managed it too. The lids were carefully placed on top and the bemused hoodies left, promising to be back by 6.00 a.m. in the morning to load the empty coffins back into the hearse.

Emma shook her perplexed head, switched the lights off and went to bed.

# CHAPTER 8

At 3.00 a.m. the night was at its sleepiest. The moon was playing cat and mouse with the clouds when the sound of slowly driven tyres on gravel whispered into the silent Bucket Street.

Mr Shorty Johnson, whose credentials had been called into question, slowed the car to a standstill opposite *Crumpets* and parked it. He had come to show how a protection racket should be run, like in the old days. Once his wife's soft-top car was stationary (he was running out of cars himself), he climbed out and shut the door noiselessly.

He leaned nonchalantly against the car and lit a huge cigar. The beacon of the cigar's glow lit up his focussed, furrowed face and a huge plume of sweet-smelling white smoke hung above him in the still night air. Satisfied there was nobody about, he walked slowly across the street to the front door of *Crumpets*.

Sneering at the name he uttered, "I'll give you crumpets. Think you can make a fool out of me, do you, darlin'? Well, let me toast a few crumpets for you." And with that he pulled from a deep pocket in his coat an old-fashioned bottle firebomb.

He pulled a long draught on the cigar and lit the fuse. It fizzed and smoked menacingly in his hand. Satisfied, he bent down and slid the fizzing firebomb through Emma's large, low letterbox. He watched it roll onto the welcome mat, continuing to fizz. Content, he turned and walked slowly and confidently back towards his wife's car. Arrogantly, he muttered to himself, 'Still a real pro, not lost me old touch. The old boys would be proud of me.'

It was when he was nearly back to the car, he first heard it. A gentle tinkling noise like dripping rain. At first, he thought it was his wife's ludicrously large keyring of trinkets jangling. But now holding it tightly in his hand, it made no noise at all. The tinkling noise was coming from behind him. A noise like a bottle rolling. It couldn't be! There was no way it could be...

The sound was very faint, but it was there and getting louder. He nervously spun around, looking everywhere behind him. He couldn't see anything. He assumed he had been mistaken and continued walking slowly towards the car. Then he felt something touch the back of his shoe.

Impossible! he thought anxiously. He looked down, not wanting it to be what he thought it might be, but it was. It was his worst nightmare – the fizzing bottle firebomb that he had just put through the letterbox of *Crumpets*.

The bottle rolled past him and under his wife's car. He tried to kick it away before it went out of sight, but his dumpy legs were too short to connect. He struggled to kneel down but just managed to peer under her car. The bottle had come to a stop exactly in the centre. The fuse was now all but nonexistent, so he clumsily clambered to his feet and ran off down the street, his camel hair coat flapping behind him. He hadn't gone forty yards when Mrs Johnson's soft-top car rose about twenty feet in the air, turned over in slow motion and landed exactly back where it had been originally parked. However, now it was upside down, and an inferno!

The noise of the explosion and breaking glass was deafening and, unsurprisingly, woke the entire street. Lights came on inside every house and residents came out in their pyjamas and dressing gowns to investigate.

Running downstairs, Emma found Arthur and Martha watching out of one of the café's bay windows. Martha had her arm around Arthur's waist and Arthur had his arm around Martha's shoulders while they watched the blaze outside.

Emma looked around. The coffin lids were closed. She didn't understand. Had they gone and come back? Had they not gone at all?

Arthur and Martha both sensed she was there and turned around at the same time to face her, smiling sheepishly. Emma anxiously rushed over to them to make sure they hadn't been hurt in the explosion. Arthur reassured her that they were both well. Emma gave them both a hug and said she couldn't bear the thought of anything happening to them. Martha reassured her again and again that they were both fine.

Within minutes, police cars and fire engines arrived and there was pandemonium in the street as water hoses were run out and the street cordoned off.

Arthur then felt an explanation was necessary. "We both heard Shorty Johnson arrive when he came to fire-bomb

*Crumpets.* So, we quickly climbed out of our coffins to do whatever was needed to prevent the inevitable explosion. It was at that precise moment when the car was ablaze and we had prevented another disaster to the café that we realised we would never see each other again. The last few weeks have been the most exciting ever for us." Martha took over from Arthur, "It was then we realised we had missed our one and only chance. But do you know what? Neither of us minded as long as we were together."

Holding both of Emma's hands, Martha pleaded, "Oh, please, may we stay with you? Please, please?"

Emma hugged the two of them again. "Of course you can stay. Stay for as long as you like. Stay as my guests. I love having you both here. It wouldn't be the same without you."

Two very happy spooks promised to be back later and left.

Emma set about making teas, coffees and bacon cobs for the police and the fire services; it looked like it was going to be a busy night.

Eventually, the fire engines with their flashing blue lights disappeared in the night. Then a low loader with its flashing orange lights came, loaded Shorty Johnson's wife's burnt-out car and took it away. Then finally, only when they couldn't eat another bacon cob, the police left too. When all was clear, a hearse with no lights on at all came and went.

———

*Crumpets* was opened the next day and closed at the normal time. All the customers could talk about was Shorty's wife's car.

The day was busier than ever.

By closing time, Emma was nearly on her knees but still there were things to do. She swept the café through, mopped the floor and repositioned the tables ready for the morning. Then she heard a tap at the door. Emma spun around, her heart in her mouth. So far, every time she had opened the door after closing time it had ended in trouble. However, she was feeling a little less anxious as she unlocked the door to Dan.

"Do you want to hear some really good news?" said Dan with a huge grin on his face.

"I would love to hear any good news for its been a bit scarce recently," replied Emma seriously.

"Shorty Johnson has left the area taking his wife and thugs with him. He was heard to say that he was moving to Spain that afternoon because of the vandalism to his cars."

She looked up from mopping the floor with tears in her eyes and said, "That really is great news. You have just put £100 a week back on my bottom line. Let me give you a big hug."

They hugged tightly and then Dan replied with, "I'd love to stop and celebrate but I've a meeting with my accountant and I'm late already. He will be delighted with the news. I thought you'd like to know as soon as I heard." Hesitantly Dan added, "But I have time for another hug."

"Thank you, thank you again. I wasn't sure how long I could keep going paying £100 every week." sobbed Emma hugging him tightly again.

Dan left her to finish mopping the floor and pulled the door shut on his way out into the rainy night.

Shortly after there was another rapping on the door. Maybe Dan had forgotten something she thought. The hoodies had been fed and watered and had long since gone, so it probably wouldn't be them either. Martha and Arthur weren't due back for ages yet and they didn't need keys anyway. Despite the good news Emma was nervous as to who it could be.

She put the security chain on the door and gingerly opened it, leaving the security chain on. She peered through the gap into the dark wet night. It took a while for her eyes to focus. There standing in the rain and offering up a bottle of wine and a take-away meal for two was Dave. Emma couldn't believe her eyes.

"I've come for the pot washer's job, if you'll have me?" He smiled apprehensively.

# CHAPTER 9

A very tired Emma stared at Dave for a full thirty seconds before unhitching the security chain, turning, walking back inside the café and leaving the door open without saying a word.

Dave cautiously followed her, astounded by the absolute transformation from the last time he saw the dirty, dusty building on that dreary night about nine months ago. He placed the bottle of wine and the carrier bag of food on a red gingham covered table by the door and shadowed her towards the counter, keeping his distance.

Emma finally snapped.

"You've got a bloody nerve, Dave." She turned and shook her head. "You really have." She looked straight at him brushing the strands of hair off her face. "When I really needed you here by my side, what was it you said? Well, let me remind you in case you've forgotten. You said to me, 'You'd better go off and do your own thing and I'll do mine.'" She emphasised every word really slowly for effect. "Well, I hope you've had a ball doing your own thing."

Dave stammered, "Look, Em, I–I'm sorry. I–"

"Shut up, Dave!" Emma interrupted and his head went down.

"What was it you went on to say? 'Go off and do your own thing. If you stay here with me, you'll always blame me for preventing you living your dream.' That's what you said, wasn't it? So, I went off and I did my own thing, and it was tough, bloody tough. Tougher than anything I could have imagined. I had no idea what I was letting myself in for BUT I DID IT!"

Emma paused her rant and just stared at him. He remained sheepish, shuffling his feet.

"Yes, on my own! Just me, no one else," she continued. "There were days when I worked so hard, I fell asleep in that old chair in the bay window because I was too tired to get up the stairs." She pointed at the high-backed winged chair.

Wincing at the tirade, Dave looked at the chair imagining her slumped in it. But she hadn't finished, oh no, there was more to come, much more. Emma was taking the skin off his back with her tongue, layer by painful layer!

"And where were you when I had to convince the skinflint of a bank manager, who has a brother called Marley, to loan me the refurb money? Where were you then? And where were you when I had to negotiate with the contractors – Sid the builder, Sparky the electrician and Micky Dripping the plumber, all of whom would only work for cash-in-hand and staged payments?" Emma touched her nose to emphasise the nature of some of the dubious deals she had so painfully learned how to seal. "And then the whole street lost power for two days. Yes, two whole days without power, not a flicker in the whole area. That was a bit of a bummer, I can tell you. I had to cook out in the backyard on two barbeques under borrowed umbrellas because it was raining cats and dogs. I had to boil water on camping gas stoves and put candles on all the tables because I couldn't afford to lose the income, not for one day. NOT FOR ONE DAY! Money was that tight. You have no idea."

Emma's voice was getting perceptibly louder as she related the litany of disasters she had coped with on her own. Dave was shuffling about wishing he was somewhere else... anywhere else. This wasn't such a good idea after all.

"And where were you when I first opened the café and the local youths were congregating on the other side of the street? Local hoodies who weren't allowed in any of the high street shops. I looked around to see if anyone would come with little five foot three inch me to meet them, but you weren't here!"

Dave tried to interject but she was clearly not going to give him an inch. Emma talked over him.

"Now it gets really serious! Where were you when two of the local thugs barged their way in and started to smash the place up because I objected to paying their protection money? Yes, little old *Crumpets* was being forced to pay a protection firm. That's when I really needed you, Dave, but you weren't here, were you? No, you were off doing your own thing, weren't you?"

Dave shuffled from one foot to another, looking at his shoes.

Emma needed a drink, a big drink. All the time she had been talking, she had been absently pouring chilled white wine into a balloon glass, and as she recalled incident after incident, tears of tiredness and temper were running freely down her flushed cheeks. Then she turned on him with her final onslaught... her crescendo!

"And worst of all, do you want to know what frightened me the most? Not what made me nervous, not what worried me a bit, but actually what made me fear for my life? Well, whether you want to hear it or not, you're going to hear it anyway." She turned to face him square on. "The worst problem of all was when the local Mafia tried to firebomb *Crumpets!*"

Emma trembled, letting her words sink in.

Dave stood open mouthed.

"Yes, you heard right. They came to post a firebomb through the letterbox of my little café. In the middle of the night." She said the words really slowly, getting louder with each one. "Yes, me, little old Emma, on my own, had to protect my... how did you describe it? My 'doomed to fail' café. Where were you, eh? Where were you then, Dave?" She practically shouted the final sentence.

Unable to look her in the eye, Dave started to mumble his previously well-rehearsed apology.

"Look, Em, I never... I'm..."

She moved towards him, sobbing. "Shut up, Dave, and kiss me," she said. "Kiss me properly. I've missed you like hell."

# CHAPTER 10

That night was frantic. After nine months apart, they didn't fall asleep in each other's arms till well after midnight.

Emma opened her eyes at the usual time on Monday morning and despite the early start, insisted they began the day with sleepy sex followed by toast and coffee in bed; something they both loved. This meant the rest of the morning was a rush.

Dave had to run to work but promised to return later.

Years previously, Dave had two school friends, Henry and Rupert, whose names accurately conveyed the type of private school they attended better than any words. To put Dave through this same prestigious school and give him the best possible chance in life his parents had made many sacrifices, such as UK camping holidays and only small Christmas presents rather than extravagance.

Following school, Dave elected to move into the financial world and went to university, exiting five years later fully qualified. His parents had no regrets and were rightly proud when they could eventually refer to their son as an accountant. It was their sacrifices that had motivated Dave after university to higher levels of academic performance than even he believed possible.

Henry and Rupert had also pursued tertiary education in the financial world. They qualified and secured positions in the venture capital market place, finally setting up their own small business together.

The three kept in touch through the obligatory continuing professional development sessions. Strangely, despite migrating to universities across the country, the three friends had returned to within thirty miles of each other. Their geographic closeness was not mirrored by their ethical closeness, which had diversified significantly.

By lunchtime, Emma was on her knees although Dave did come back as promised and their second evening together was more sensibly paced. They chatted until late, becoming really serious about the future.

"How about this for a plan then?" suggested Dave, "I work my notice period and leave my accountancy job but keep on working for a couple of clients in Ireland privately. They'll be happy to keep me on and I'll save them a shed load of money if I work direct. If the café takes a financial nosedive for a few weeks then the Irish money might come in handy. I'll need to go there once or twice every six weeks to keep them sweet. What do you think?"

"Seems OK so far." Emma nodded.

"I keep the flat on and stay there to ensure we both get some sleep rather than jostle all night over space in your micro bed." He nudged her playfully. Emma coloured up a bit. "I'll spend the weekends here with you if that's OK?" Dave suggested.

Emma nodded again.

He continued, "I'll work in the café and when there is a quiet time I'll do the books." Emma didn't need long to let someone take over the books for even after all the time she had been doing them they might as well be written in Swahili. It would be like having her own fairy god mother.

Despite this amazing offer her sensible head dropped into gear, "Let's agree on a trial period of twelve months, then we can review how things are working out from a romantic perspective and a working perspective. If either of us believe it's not working then we part company with no hard feelings. What do you think?"

Dave replied, "I'm in."

———

Unknown to Emma, in the background, as soon as Henry and Rupert heard Dave had left his job at the accountancy firm, they invited him to join their little business. Dave chose to stick with *Crumpets*.

Four weeks later Dave's first day at *Crumpets* did not start well despite him being there on the dot of 6.30 a.m. He adamantly refused to wear a 'pinny'. Emma already had twelve months experience dealing with difficult people under her belt and head on was her final style.

After twenty minutes of suggesting alternatives, she had Dave wearing a full-length apron in the style of a Parisian maître d'. Emma smiled to herself every time she noticed him mincing about the café catching glances of himself in the mirrors. He kept his stomach in tight and tensed his bum when he walked. She wondered if he would still be mincing at the end of a busy day. She also wondered if his intransigence over trivial things would manifest itself in other ways and battles would be frequent.

The bell on the door jangled announcing the early risers, and into the café tumbled four white van drivers playfully jostling to get to the counter first. Dave stood there in his important apron, pen and pad in hand.

"Who are you? Where's Emma? You the new boss? Are you two an item?" The questions were machine-gunned at him.

"I'm Dave and here to help out."

"And I thought you were going to marry me, Emma," one of them shouted into the kitchen.

"You're already married and have dozens of kids, or had you forgotten?" Emma called back.

"Yeah, you're right, I'd forgotten about the wife."

"Usual?" she shouted.

"Yeah, with extra chips," called another.

"Same old joke every morning. You know we don't do chips for breakfast."

They sat down noisily at a table.

Dave went into the kitchen and asked Emma what was he to charge them. Did she have a two-tier charging system for locals or mates' rates?

"No, everything is as shown on the blackboard with no exceptions. They know the prices to the penny and will put it on the counter before they go," Emma assured him.

"You sure?"

"Absolutely."

By the time he had returned to the counter he was surprised to see a queue of noisy workmen had formed. He took the new orders as best he could then conveyed them to Emma who immediately handed him four plates piled high with cooked breakfasts.

"This one's for the gobby one who wants to marry me and this one is for the smallest one who they call Big Willie and before you ask, I don't know. This one is for the one in green overalls and this one is for Snoz. I don't know why he's called Snoz either."

"How much do I charge them?" queried Dave again.

Emma sighed. "Dave, you have no need to worry about the prices. They always pay before they leave and I charge exactly what's up on the blackboard."

"What if they don't?"

"I've already told you they will."

Dave served teas and coffees to the four white-van-drivers and they were silent as they devoured their food at Olympic speed. Four handfuls of coins were placed on the counter as the four white-van-drivers left, all belching and shouting bye to Emma.

Dave felt invisible.

By the time 6.00 pm eventually arrived, Dave sat down exhausted. He hadn't even had time for a coffee in eleven and a half hours. Neither had Emma.

"Two more jobs, Dave. Chairs on the tables then sweep through and mop the floor. Then bring the outside tables and chairs inside and please don't forget to wipe them down." Dave nodded wearily.

While putting the chairs on the tables, the door jangled and three hoodies entered the café.

"We're closed!" shouted a very tired Dave.

"Where's Emma?" asked Jumbo.

"Didn't you hear me? We're closed. Out you go. Come back tomorrow or next week or the next decade. Right now, we're closed, got it?"

The hoodies hesitated and started retreating. Emma appeared from the kitchen.

"What are you doing, Dave? These are my friends. I'll put some pizzas on."

Jumbo and Bean sat down at their regular table and Mollie went behind the counter to grab some Cokes. Dave watched her every move, keeping his eyes on her and the till.

After Emma had introduced everyone properly, the conversation was stilted. A new dynamic had been introduced into the café. Nobody was comfortable.

To lighten the moment Jumbo asked, "Spooks comin'?"

Three kicks under the table suggested this was an inappropriate question for today.

# CHAPTER 11

To be fair to Dave, over the six weeks, he did work hard in the café, but insisted on taking the books home because as soon as he started getting to grips with Emma's quaint accounting systems, customers seemed to know and came flocking in.

Dave also encouraged Emma get out of the café to see how other cafés were working. Occasionally, she took the opportunity and returned with lots of ideas. Things seemed to be moving in the right direction for both of them.

One evening, when Dave had taken the books home early, Emma asked Arthur and Martha, Jumbo, Bean and Mollie round for supper. She wanted it to be just like the old days when there was just her, the three hoodies and her two live-in spooks. She had decided not to tell Dave about Arthur and Martha just yet. As a practical accountant, she felt sure he would not cope well with the idea of the spirit world.

Soon, laughter raised the roof at *Crumpets* and the old buzz made Emma feel complete. It was such a wonderful feeling. The Cokes were flowing, the pizzas were flying off the plates and stories of Bucket Street were being told along with comparisons of what it was like in the old days to where it is now.

Arthur produced his tin of snuff, which was always a delight to the hoodies as they could not comprehend why anyone would want to push ground tobacco up their nose. Having each tried it once before and sneezed their heads off, they all declined 'a pinch'.

Martha dismissed it as a filthy habit and pinched her little posh nose, which led to roars of laughter from the hoodies all trying to imitate her. Martha didn't mind a bit and sometimes exaggerated her posh accent for fun.

Arthur dismissed her criticism as his, 'only vice'.

"Wine?" asked Bean.

"Well, that's just for medicinal purposes you understand," countered Arthur, shushing Bean playfully.

Emma could not have been more pleased with the light-hearted banter between youth and age at the table. The incredulously archaic stories of the local schools had them enthralled, compared to today where the cane and the slipper were historic teaching tools and every child knew their rights. This was the best evening she had for such a long time. Well, nearly the best... She blushed at the memory of her and Dave's reunion. Tonight, she needed to be surrounded by her friends.

It was the best evening until Jumbo innocently asked the question, "What's all this I've heard about the council knocking Bucket Street down to make a bypass for the High Street?

Silence descended on the café.

Jumbo felt he had to explain. "My mum works as a cleaner in the council planning office and saw the plans. Please don't say anything. I shouldn't 'ave mentioned it. She'll get the sack if it gets out."

They all nodded their promises but Emma felt sick.

Arthur then added in a very serious tone, "I'm afraid it's true, Emma. We've only heard rumours from our friends and wanted to get more information on the council's plans before we said anything to you."

Martha took over, "Arthur's right, my dear. We've only heard bits and pieces and hearsay, but I'm afraid what little we do know gets worse. Apparently, a development company has already bought up six houses here on Bucket Street, each for a song. I'm sure their plan is to buy as many as they can. Eventually, the council will have to make compulsory purchase orders on all the properties they want to demolish. The development company will make a killing. They have already made the butcher next door an offer."

"How do I not know anything about this?" Emma shook her head in disbelief. "I run a café in the middle of the street that's going to be knocked down!"

"It's because there's the opportunity for a few people to make a financial killing as long as nobody knows anything about it. If the plan gets out to Bucket Street home owners, nobody will sell to the development company. They'll wait for the compulsory purchase orders. If Bucket Street home owners are not aware of the plans and do sell to the development company, they will be frightened into secrecy until all the legals have been completed."

"Exactly what is happening? You said 'it gets worse.' How can it be worse?" asked a confused Emma who was trying to hold back tears. "*Crumpets* will be bulldozed to the ground. What could be worse than that?"

"I'm sorry, Emma, but where it gets worse is we've heard that the company buying up the houses is called Seren Ltd. and run by two of Dave's friends, Henry and Rupert."

Emma felt sick. She had met these two so-called friends of Dave, and instantly disliked them both. Why Dave had palled up with them was beyond her. She sat with her head in her hands not saying a word.

The hoodies understood the significance of the conversation and Jumbo started to quietly clear the dishes away, wishing he had never said anything.

Mollie and Bean also helped then Emma looked up and said, "Not a word to anyone please. Let's get some more information and then decide what do."

Arthur, Martha and the three hoodies all understood.

———

Emma had a dreadful night. How could the council do it? How could Dave not have told her? She couldn't fight them all, could she? A hundred questions swirled in her mind as she watched her café go round and round a nightmare plughole and then down the drain. A bulldozed dream. Just bricks and rubble to be covered in tarmac. She cried and cried.

When Dave arrived the next day, he immediately knew something was wrong. The atmosphere was icy.

"Well, when were you going to tell me?" snapped Emma, unable to contain herself a second longer.

"Tell you what?"

"About your plans with Henry and Rupert?"

"What plans?"

"To buy up Bucket Street houses before the compulsory purchase orders were served to build the bypass."

"I haven't got a clue about what you are talking about."

"Is that why you came back?" she asked.

"No. They did ask me to join them, but I came back to be with you, here at *Crumpets*."

"Did they ask you to come back so you could soften me up before they made an offer."

"No, no. I know they run a small venture capital company, but that's it. I'll ring them and find out the truth."

"No, you won't. You'll tip them off if you're not involved and if you are, you can pack now!"

The doorbell jangled, announcing customers.

"We'll talk later," snapped Emma, close to tears again.

Upstairs in her tiny flat at the end of the day Dave joined Emma.

"How can I trust you now?" asked Emma in tears.

"Because I haven't done anything wrong." replied Dave quietly

"But your friends have. They're fleecing all the folk in Bucket Street. Honest people who believed in me when I first started. Without them I would never have got *Crumpets* off the ground."

"But I'm not fleecing anyone! Rupert and Henry are, according to you. I told you, I'm not involved."

"You're all tarred with the same brush; Rupert, Henry and you! You went to school together, you went to college together, you all live close together, and they offered you a job as soon as they heard you were about to leave your old accountancy firm."

"Yes, they did offer me a job to join them. It came out of the blue. I said no thanks. Apart from Continuing Professional Development, which I have to go to for my qualification, I rarely see either of them."

"Be honest, did they offer you money to try and soften me up to sell when the time came?" asked Emma.

"That's a really below the belt remark and says something about the way you feel about me," Dave said, with a disappointed scowl. "To answer you, no they didn't ask me to soften you up, and I would have thought that by working twelve hours a day in *Crumpets* I would have demonstrated that I am pretty committed. But that doesn't seem enough for you, does it? Well, I'm not sure I know what else to say, other than tell you one more time that I have nothing to do with either Rupert or Henry, or what they are up to. However, I will tell you one thing and that is that if they are investing heavily in a money-making venture, they will have researched it thoroughly, and they will make a shed-load of money out of it. So, as there seems nothing else to say I'm off to look for a job where, when things go wrong, I'm not the first to be blamed."

"Surely you can see how it looks?" Emma pleaded.

"I don't give a toss about how it looks," he snapped.

I'm sorry, Dave," she apologised. "I'm just so stressed about the news."

"Well, look for someone else who will work twelve hours a day and who is happy to be your whipping boy when you get stressed. It's not me."

"Please don't go like this. I've said I'm sorry." Emma reached for his hand but he moved it away.

"Your last comment that I would have taken money to soften you up to sell was the final straw. I'm off."

With that, Dave stomped down the narrow stairs and slammed the flat door shut then let himself out of the café. Emma cried herself to sleep.

The following morning, she was up early and had most of the jobs done so that if he did come back, and she really doubted that he would, they could talk.

To her relief, Dave did come back and apologised for his part of the evening row and for having such crappy, dishonest friends. Emma led him up to her flat and apologised too, for doubting him. Without talking any more, they made up as she hoped they would.

———

The next night Emma, Arthur and Martha met to try to plan what could be done. As far as they could see it, there were two things to do. 1. Stop Henry and Rupert and 2. Stop the council.

Emma asked Arthur and Martha to stop Henry and Rupert. They were to find as much information as possible about them as possible. Athur and Martha would illicit the research from all their close spirit friends and acquaintances. Emma said she would ask some of her regulars, in a round-about way, about what they had heard. Someone would surely know something about six houses having been purchased in Bucket Street?

---

Over the next few days, Emma innocently asked a few customers how much the houses in Bucket Street were going for. Just by chance, one of the owners then came into the café for his coffee and toasted tea-cake. He had fallen on hard times a couple of months previously and Emma had given him a few meals to tide him over so he was happy to share everything with her; the amount, the timing and the special conditions.

"Special conditions?" probed Emma.

"Yes, I'm not supposed to say a word about the offer to anyone. If I do the offer will be revoked immediately. Apparently, it's something to do with tax. I didn't understand."

Emma shared her findings with Arthur and Martha that night.

Using their many friends, Arthur and Martha had found out that Henry's diary was populated by a number of covert Seren Ltd. development meetings interspersed with the occasional mundane appointments to the dentist and optician. A normal businessman's busy agenda.

An optician's appointment was scheduled for the next afternoon. They decided that this would be their target and agreed to report back the following night. In the meantime,

Emma would continue to find out everything she could about the property purchases in Bucket Street.

The next day, Arthur and Martha positioned themselves in a small coffee shop on the opposite side of the road to the optician's. This was the wealthy end of town. They watched Henry saunter into the building exactly on time.

Inside the optician's the pretty receptionist smiled at Henry, which he arrogantly interpreted as her being attracted to him. After only the briefest of exchanges he invited her out, only to receive a curt and robust rebuff. Without any further conversation, she led him into the optician's surgery for his eye test.

As he expected, all the results were favourable from the first test. The Snellen chart to measure visual acuity was next. The optician patiently explained the purpose of the test.

"I've always had 20/20 vision so please just get on with it as I have a busy schedule for the day," an impatient Henry replied.

Without any glasses he quickly read:

I

FYO

UCON

TINUEW

ITHBYP

ASSPLA

NSYOUWI

LLENDUPBR

OKE

The optician looked at him incredulously.

"What?" asked Henry. "I told you – 20/20 vision. Perfect. I'm amazing." He started getting out of the chair.

"Will you read it again for me, please, sir?" asked the optician.

"Why?"

"Because you did not get one letter right! Not one! So, please, read it again."

Exasperated, Henry looked at his watch then started to read again. The optician wrote down exactly what Henry read back to him.

"There, letter perfect, 20/20," Henry repeated his own self-assessment.

The optician passed him the sheet of paper showing what he had recorded.

Henry went over to the Snellen chart with the paper and compared the two. Embarrassed and confused, he came out in a real sweat.

"I must be having a bad day. I'll make another appointment," he mumbled and, taking the sheet of paper with him, swiftly left, not even acknowledging the receptionist.

That night Henry insisted Rupert join him for a drink in a pub. Henry was in a real state and close to a breakdown. Having shown Rupert the optician's sheet of paper and a copy of the Snellen chart, he waited for an explanation.

Rupert shrugged.

"Maybe it's a bad dream and tomorrow you'll hardly be able to remember any of it?"

Henry wasn't convinced.

"It's not a bloody bad dream, as you so flippantly say. Have you read what it says?"

"Well, it's the same old random letters we all get, isn't it?"

"No, it's not! It says: IF YOU CONTINUE WITH YOUR PLANS FOR THE BYPASS YOU WILL END UP BROKE.

"Wow, I didn't notice that first time around. I see now why you're a bit upset." Rupert sat back, also visibly shaken. "It's probably some subliminal conscience warning you to be careful."

"A bit upset? What do you mean 'a bit upset'? I'm shaken to the bloody core. It's not warning *me*, as you said, it's warning *us*. Do you think it's a premonition and we ought to cut our losses and pull out?" asked Henry.

"Certainly not!" snapped Rupert. "I've invested everything I have in this and I'm not pulling out now. We'll get the butcher's, next we'll get the newsagents and then we'll get Dave to help with the café when he's not chasing off to Dublin. We'll be on the top of our credit level. Just trust me, this is the really nervy end of the deal."

With that Rupert ordered two more shorts, finished his and left, leaving Henry to pay.

That evening, Arthur and Martha reported Henry's appointment back to Emma. She was impressed, "Why you sly pair, I would never have thought of that. I'd love to have seen his face when he realised what he'd read out.

What have you got up your sleeves next?"

"Tonight, we'll go for Rupert, the cocky one."

Rupert, the CEO of Seren Ltd. had fallen fast asleep in bed that night with the light on, following a cocktail of wine and worry. Pages and pages of the company's financial information were strewn all over the bed and some had slipped onto the floor of his huge bachelor bedroom. A wine glass half full of heady red wine stood on the bedside cabinet and the remnants of a partly eaten takeaway sandwich was smeared over one of his many pillows. This was one disturbed business man.

"Perfect," said Arthur as he positioned Martha and one of their spirit friends on Rupert's dining room chairs, placed beside the acre of bed.

Arthur and another friend then sat on the other two chairs on the opposite side. The bed had doubled up as a boardroom table. A sleeping Rupert occasionally snored at its head.

Before the meeting began, the four of them looked around the bedroom to get a measure of the person with whom they were dealing. It was a typical, single man's bedroom with clothes strewn everywhere. Dumb bells and men's magazines littered the corners of the room. Used coffee cups jostled dirty wine glasses for space on the narrow shelf above the padded headboard. A confusion of smells lingered in the room, one, two, maybe three recent perfumes, killer aftershave and deodorant. However, the most pungent smell came from a pair of old trainers by the side of the bed. Arthur kicked them well under.

On every set of drawers sat a selection of half burnt candles, but what intrigued them most was the large mirror positioned directly over the bed. When Martha first spotted it she tutted loudly, causing the other three to look up. Arthur growled something about 'morals of modern youth'.

Their spirit lady friend whispered a question to the fourth spirit. "Why would anyone install a mirror on the ceiling? It must be so inconvenient to brush your hair and one would have to stand on the bed to put lipstick on. I'm sure I'd smudge mine everywhere on this bouncy mattress."

The fourth spirit smiled patiently, trying to imagine her bouncing.

Another even louder tut, tut came from Martha, accompanied by her shaking her head.

When Arthur, Martha and their two friends had straightened some of the papers on the bed and were settled, they all became visible.

Arthur started the meeting by talking quite loudly. "Let's start by confirming what we know." The other three spirits nodded.

Arthur continued, "We know that after soliciting information from a variety of sources, a company called Seren Ltd. discovered that the council had advanced plans to build a bypass for the High Street. One suggestion tabled, in secret, in the council was to demolish part of Bucket Street to facilitate the bypass. This proposal probably included demolishing all the properties from number 60 Bucket Street, on both sides of the street down to the High Street. This proposal would definitely include the butcher's, the newsagent's and *Crumpets*. Having discovered this plan, Seren Ltd. has been buying up poor quality housing in Bucket Street in the way of the proposed bypass plan. So far, they have acquired six houses from unsuspecting owners at knock-down prices. Plans for three more purchases are well under way."

The four of them only looked at Rupert when sleep apnoea interrupted the rhythm of his slumber. He stirred now.

Rupert, aware that something wasn't right, could hear voices, but was not yet awake enough to focus. He was listening to people talking on the other side of a wall of consciousness. However, the conversation was becoming clearer as the bricks were being removed one by one.

"So, the objective of this meeting," said Arthur, "is to determine if the two partners of Seren Ltd. – Henry and Rupert – are guilty of insider trading, deceit, fraud or all three."

Martha had just started to present her thoughts to the meeting when Rupert suddenly opened his eyes.

He jerked, looking around the bed, not understanding what was happening. "Am I in hospital?" he questioned.

"No, you are not in hospital," replied Arthur.

"Have I been in an accident?" anxiously asked Rupert.

"No, there are no white coats. No, this isn't a dream," said Arthur

Rupert sat upright abruptly.

"Who the f*** are you?" he demanded. He was just about to throw back the duvet and get out of bed then remembered he slept in the nude and thought better of it.

Arthur snapped at him. "Do not use language like that again in my meeting! Do you understand, young man? You are in enough trouble already."

Shocked, Rupert sat back, covered his chest up with the duvet and feebly apologised. He was now totally confused. This was his bedroom, his bed, his house. These were his dining room chairs from downstairs with strangers sat on them having a meeting about his company. He looked at the four people in turn. He didn't know any of them, but they had been talking knowledgably about Seren Ltd. They had been talking about what was happening at this very moment, which was supposed to be a secret! Outside of the council, only he and Henry knew about the plans. His brain was trying to re-run the conversation he had heard in his sleep before waking properly. He shook his head to clear his thoughts. It made no difference.

Arthur continued, "The second objective of this meeting is to decide if we should inform the council of Seren Ltd.'s behaviour. They will definitely take action. Or, should we inform the fraud squad, who will definitely take action. Or, should we inform the financial regulatory body who will strike the directors of Seren Ltd. off any professional accounting bodies, prohibiting them from practicing in the future. Perhaps we should inform all three?"

Mumbles from all present focussed Rupert's mind. He shivered. This could be the end of his career. He pulled the duvet up higher to his chin. More papers spilled onto the floor.

Martha then asked, "Is the real question, Mr Chairman, did they know they were doing wrong?"

Arthur suggested she ask him and the four turned towards Rupert as one.

"Well, young man, did you know you were doing wrong when you embarked upon buying poor peoples' homes before they were aware they would shortly be offered more generous compulsory purchase orders?"

Rupert, now completely awake, started to formulate a round-about explanation then stopped himself. "Before I continue, could you tell me who all of you actually are?"

Arthur agreed. "A reasonable question." He looked around the group for agreement. It was unanimous.

"We, young man, are a group of people who will not tolerate poor people being exploited i.e. poor people whose homes you have bought for only half their real value. We are a group of people who deplore social deprivation and the subjugation of the elderly or infirm by people like you for your personal financial gain. We are a group of people who correct injustices. Enough?"

Feeling guilty, Rupert shrugged his shoulders. "What do you want me to do?"

Arthur started, "We don't *want* you to do anything. We *insist* you do the following: 1. Withdraw your offer to the butcher at 54 Bucket Street. 2. Pull out of the existing six house purchases and offer them all £1,000 compensation. 3. Make a donation of £20,000 to build Bucket Street Primary School a playground between *Crumpets* and the High Street where the bypass was planned to run. Make the offer in the local paper anonymously. And this is all to be completed by Friday. Five days. Is that clear?"

Arthur pushed a sheet of paper with the terms across the duvet to Rupert.

He nodded. "Perfectly."

Arthur smiled. "Any other business?" he asked. There was none. "Then that will be all. The meeting is now closed."

As one, the four spirits disappeared leaving Rupert shaking in his bed and in no doubt of what needed to be done... by Friday.

An hour later, he was beginning to doubt what had happened, but the sheet of terms and conditions was still on top of his duvet and four dining room chairs were still around his bed.

———

At *Crumpets*, Arthur and Martha reported back to Emma.

"Do you think he will do what you have asked?" she queried as she sipped a well-earned glass of chilled white wine in her dressing gown.

"We don't know, but we'll stay close to the two of them for the next couple of days," replied Martha, clearly in a very focussed mode.

"Yes, this is too important to leave to chance and we're dealing with some very slippery people here." Arthur poured more wine for himself and Martha.

"Do you think we could ask Jumbo's mum if any council developments are happening in the near future that would influence the decision?" asked Emma.

"We would be putting her job at risk," Martha reminded her. "And introducing someone else into the equation. You would also have to declare to her how you know and that would compromise Jumbo. I don't think you would want that."

"No, no certainly not. I'm not thinking clearly, it's late. Forget I suggested the idea," said Emma.

# CHAPTER 12

The next day, Arthur and Martha split up to follow Henry and Rupert, who had just three days left to execute Arthur's demands.

Dave continued to work hard in the café and kept his promise not to contact either Henry or Rupert about their shady 'business' dealings.

By now, Mollie had left school despite the other two hoodies, the spooks and Emma all trying to persuade her to stay but she was adamant and the day after her last day of the Christmas half-term holiday she was sixteen and started to work in *Crumpets* full time. Jumbo and Bean agreed she was in charge now and began calling her 'boss', laughing every time they said it.

"Yes, boss. No, boss," they said to her whenever she asked them anything.

It made Mollie smile.

Emma was stressed at the thought of potentially losing her café, despite Mollie and Dave taking some of the daily work strain from her. She had hardly been sleeping at night and often made mistakes, one after another, as she did whenever she was under pressure.

Mollie was becoming concerned about her.

Coincidentally, Dan the butcher asked to speak to Emma privately when there was a quiet moment in the café.

"I just wanted to share something with you. I have been made an offer for my shop and I've been mulling it over for the last couple of weeks. I'm not sure what to do. If someone had offered me six pence for my shop before you breezed into Bucket Street and took it by storm with *Crumpets*, I would have snapped their hand off, locked up and gone travelling."

Emma let him continue, knowing how this was going to affect so many other folk.

"But Bucket Street has come alive since you arrived, you have made my decision to sell really difficult."

"I'm sorry," she said.

"No, please, I love the buzz of the place and both the newsagent and I have benefited significantly since *Crumpets* opened. I just don't know what to do and wanted to chat it over with you. If that's alright?"

"Of course it's alright. I'm flattered you want to confide in me." Emma smiled but she was embarrassed that she knew what was happening in the street and he didn't. He had helped her create *Crumpets*' reputation with his meat, without which she would definitely not have the following of customers she enjoyed. "Look," she said, "I'm going to tell you something about what is happening here. But please promise me you won't tell anyone yet."

"I promise."

"Well, a group of financial people in a company named Seren Ltd. have found out that the Council will be knocking the houses and our shops down to build a bypass around the town. They are buying up everything they can in the hope of making a financial killing."

Dan became angry at this point and was all for storming into the council offices to confront everyone over the matter. Emma calmed him down and continued. With her hand on his arm she pleaded with him to wait till Friday before he made a decision. "OK, I trust that you know what you're doing and promise to wait till Friday. Thank you, Emma."

He put his arms around her, gave her a hug and said, "It's me who needs to thank you. I could have made a terrible mistake."

"No decision till after Friday, OK?" repeated Emma. He nodded.

———

At closing time on Thursday, Arthur and Martha appeared solemn faced.

"That Rupert is a thoroughly disreputable individual," said a red-faced Arthur crossly.

Martha snapped, "And Henry's no better either."

Emma had to pacify the pair of them with tea and buttered toast before either could speak properly.

Thirty minutes later, Arthur explained. "As you are aware, my role this week has been to tail Rupert in the shadows, which I have executed with alacrity, even though I do say so myself."

"Thank you, Arthur. Remember, self-praise is a hollow compliment," chided Martha, dismissively.

"You're right, my dear. As I was saying, I've been following him since we had the meeting in his bedroom. Well, he left his house early the next morning and went straight to Henry's house, where he told him he had been offered a job up north and had accepted. Henry was mad at first, but when Rupert said he wanted nothing from the partnership and would legally turn over everything to Henry, he couldn't believe his luck. Henry's avaricious side kicked into overdrive and he changed completely. It obviously meant that if the council's plan did go through, he would be the sole owner of Seren Ltd. and, overnight would become very wealthy."

Arthur sighed, believing this hand of the cards might mean they had lost the battle for *Crumpets*. Clearly exasperated he continued, "Rupert is an absolute scoundrel to do that to his partner."

"Although, I'm not sure their partnership was one made in heaven in the first place," suggested Martha caustically, cutting another helping of toast with more vim and vigour than necessary.

"Well," continued Arthur, "Henry quickly accepted Rupert's offer and they shook hands on the deal. As if by magic from his briefcase, Rupert immediately produced the transfer documents. Within a few moments Henry had signed them and his partner had witnessed them. A minute after that, Rupert was gone."

"Where does that leave us?" asked Emma.

"I'm afraid it means we were back to square one. I couldn't speak I was so very angry. In fact, I was spitting tacks," said Arthur, shaking his head.

Martha was patting and smoothing his hand to calm him down. Emma was also concerned about his high colour and his blood pressure, but had to check herself and remember that he was already dead! She wondered if it could be a problem anymore.

Returning to more pressing matters Emma asked, "So, what did you do?" She was desperate to know what possible steps could be taken to stop the inevitable now.

"Well, I couldn't just leave it there, could I? So, I followed Rupert to one of those posh cafés, waited till he had sat down with a cup of coffee and a croissant and plonked myself down opposite him. He nearly fainted. He recognised me instantly from our bedroom boardroom meeting. He tried to get out, but wouldn't touch me at any price. I don't think he thought snotty ectoplasm would enhance his Jaeger suit! Anyway, I asked how his meeting with Henry had gone and he became really agitated. I reiterated that he still had to pull out of the deal with the butcher, get out of the six house sales as well as give each £1,000 compensation and make the £20,000 donation to the school for the playground. I reminded him that if he didn't take us seriously, the council, the fraud squad and the financial regulatory body would know the minute the local paper was out, if it didn't have news about the donation on the front page."

"What did he say to that?" asked Emma.

"Well, he then smugly said, 'I no longer have anything to do with Seren Ltd. Henry owns it lock, stock and barrel now.'

He went on, quite aggressively I must say, to suggest that I could, 'get stuffed', whatever that means. Mind you, I have a pretty good idea, the bounder. He then sneered in triumph and crowed, 'So you're talking to the wrong person and here are the papers to prove it.' He rummaged in his briefcase, brandished the transfer folder of papers and flapped it open in my face. However, somehow, where Henry's signature had once been was now a smiley face. He was distraught, rummaging through the papers time and time again, looking for the signature." Arthur chuckled. "I'm afraid, Martha, I then did a silly thing, of which I'm not proud."

"Oh, no, Arthur. You didn't, did you? You'll get caught one day and then we'll all be in trouble."

"What did you do?" asked Emma, thoroughly invested in the story.

"Well, just to get his attention you understand, I made his coffee and croissant disappear. He sat back in his chair just looking between me and where they had been. His mouth and eyes were stretched open to their widest point." Arthur giggled again to himself, thrilled with his mischief. He glanced at Martha and immediately became serious and formal again.

"I went on to tell him that you, Martha, were currently at Henry's house explaining his deceit and issuing Henry with the same list of conditions that we gave to him to fulfil before this Friday. I then told Rupert that Henry was pretty upset about the meeting they had this morning and most of Henry's descriptors of Rupert's conduct were unrepeatable.

I added that just before you left, you had asked Henry how his eyes were today, thus connecting us directly with his recent optician's appointment. I told him that the colour had drained out of Henry's face and beads of sweat had run down his face.

I then made Rupert's coffee and croissant reappear, but the croissant had a big bite out of it. They really are splendid, Martha, despite the fact they are French. You must try one. We never had anything like them in our day. Rupert could not have sat further away from the plate. I really had his attention then."

"What do you think the pair of them will do now then?" wondered Emma.

"No idea, but they are both frightened witless. Let's wait till the first edition of the local paper tomorrow night. It comes out about 7.00 p.m.

———

On Friday at closing time there was a knock at the door of the café. Emma answered and was met by Jumbo and a slight woman.

"This is my mum," said Jumbo, embarrassed. "She wants to talk to you."

Emma immediately thought that Jumbo was in trouble for saying something about the bypass but she invited them in. Jumbo stayed in the café while Emma took his mum upstairs and made her a cup of tea.

"Please call me Lillian," she started. "James was often in trouble in school."

"James?" interrupted Emma curiously.

"Oh, you probably know him as Jumbo," Emma nodded towards her son. She went on to explain the reason for her visit, "Well, James, as I said, was often in trouble at school. But since he's been coming here with his two friends, he's changed completely. I sometimes don't recognise him."

Emma held her breath, waiting anxiously for the next bit, good or bad.

"Yes, he's so helpful around the house now and cooks his brother's tea, 'cos I work and can't get back for when they get home. Sometimes, when I'm on a late shift, James waits up to make sure I get home OK. And I think it's all come about because of your influence, so I wanted to come and thank you myself."

Beaming, Emma stepped in very quickly with, "He's a super lad, very courteous and helpful. You should be very proud of him. I don't know what I would have done without all three kids' company some days. After a hard day they really prop me up. I owe them a lot. It's kind of you to say that coming here has helped but basically, he's a super kid. Thank you for coming and telling me. It really means a lot to me."

Emma was desperate to ask about the bypass but decided not to, however, just as Lillian was about to leave, she said, "Good thing about the bypass, isn't it?"

Emma looked quizzically at her.

"Yes," Lillian continued, "thank the Lord, the council have finally made a decision. The bypass will only affect the houses from number 80 up to number 95 Bucket Street. Sadly, they will all have to be demolished. But that's good news for you here at number 52 isn't it? The new link from the bypass to the High Street will go right past your café. Goodness, I'm sorry, I shouldn't have said anything. I'll lose my job – please don't say a word, will you? But I was so pleased for you when I heard!" exclaimed Lillian.

Emma assured her by closing an imaginary zip across her lips and then gave her a hug for telling her the news.

Lillian added, "It's also great news about the anonymous donation to build a new playground for the school, isn't it? It's all over tonight's paper." She went on to excitedly explain how important the donation is. "Because the school is between *Crumpets* and the High Street, the council wouldn't dare change their minds and suggest bulldozing the school and its brand new playground to build a road. There would be an outright war, not only on Bucket Street itself but the surrounding catchment areas too."

"It's great news for lots of reasons!" bubbled Emma, hardly able to contain herself."

"Thanks again for everything you've done for James," said Lillian, smiling. And with that, she left.

Jumbo stayed to continue helping Mollie clear up.

No sooner had Lillian gone when there was another knock at the door. This time it was Dan and Emma welcomed him in.

"They've withdrawn their offer to me," he began, clearly desperate to tell her his news. "I can't believe it. I'm so pleased the decision has been taken away from me. I've also heard, nothing to do with what the council are doing, that the old lady in the house next door to mine wants to sell and go to live with her daughter on the other side of the town. So I'm going to put an offer in to expand my shop, which means I'll be bothering you for a long time to come, demanding coffee and toast. If that's OK?"

He smiled widely at her, looking the happiest she'd ever seen him look.

Emma was thrilled for him, gave him a big hug and said, "I'm delighted you're stopping. Where else can I get bacon as good as you sell?"

The smiling butcher left to celebrate and start planning his shop extension.

Into *Crumpets* next skipped Arthur and Martha, flourishing the local paper.

"We did it! We did it. There are three houses for sale here on Bucket Street between us and the High Street already. They must be the ones that were too far gone in the sales process to withdraw so Rupert and Henry must have immediately put them back on the market to recover some of their losses. And the front-page story is all about an anonymous gift to the school for a new playground between *Crumpets* and the High Street. It's great news. At last, we're all safe again." Arthur and Martha turned to each other and did a high five learned from the hoodies.

Emma decided it was a perfect time for a celebration. They rearranged the tables and out came bottles of wine for Emma, Arthur and Martha, with the best balloon glasses that held nearly half a bottle each. As it was a special occasion, Emma asked the hoodies if they would like a small beer. Jumbo and Bean's eyes lit up. Mollie declined in favour of her usual Coke. Smoking hot pizzas with everyone's favourite double thickness toppings were lined up, and scones, cream and strawberry jam were added to the feast. It was already a great party.

As everyone was celebrating and making lots of noise, someone popped back to the café unexpectedly...

Dave gave a stunned Emma a peck on the cheek as he passed her, waved hello to the wide-eyed and open-mouthed hoodies and headed towards the table with an outstretched hand to introduced himself to Arthur and Martha.

"Hi, my name's Dave. And you are?"

Quick as lightning, Mollie distracted him before he got to the table. "Dave, before you sit down and get introduced, please help me. The till has jammed again. We've 'ad had trouble all day and had to set up loose change floats in boxes and all sorts of things to get us through. Please can you work your magic on it again?"

"OK. Excuse me just a moment," Dave said to Arthur and Martha. He diverted over to Mollie at the counter, knelt down and started to unjam the till.

As soon as he was behind the counter and out of sight, the two spirits disappeared leaving half eaten pizzas on their plates. The half-eaten slices were snatched up by Bean and Jumbo, who devoured them instantaneously.

Emma nodded at Bean and Jumbo and then at the two full balloon glasses of red wine, they necked them in one go, facing each other. She shook her head vigorously for them to stop; she had meant for them to clear them away, not drink them!

Emma took all the now empty glasses and plates into the kitchen. That just left the two extra chairs, which she rearranged into gaps at an adjoining table. They then shuffled the remaining four chairs evenly back around the table before clearing away what was left of the crockery, Coke bottles, scones and cream.

The three of them moved deftly around the café as though clearing up as normal, ready for shutting up for the night.

Eventually, Dave poked his head above the counter.

"There, that should do it." He tried the till drawer several times to make sure it worked then he looked around the café, frowning. "Where have the two old folk gone? They were here only moments ago."

"Oh, they sometimes pop in at this time, as much for a chat as for a coffee. They never stay long," replied Emma with her fingers crossed. She walked back into the kitchen carrying some trays before shouting to Dave, "What did you forget?"

"I picked up last month's files by mistake. I need this months."

"Fancy a hot chocolate or would you like to join me in some wine and I'll tell you some very good news?" Emma called temptingly.

"I don't need good news to drink wine, but good news usually encourages a second and third glass," he called back to her.

"Bye both," shouted Mollie as she shepherded Bean and Jumbo outside, closing the café door behind them. She hurried them around the corner and away from the café where Bean was promptly sick in the gutter and Jumbo walked straight into a lamppost which made his nose bleed... then he fell over.

"What's the matter with you two?" snapped Mollie as she tried to help Jumbo up. He immediately stumbled backwards a couple of steps and fell backwards into a privet hedge.

"Never again, never, never again," groaned Bean, who was upright once more and wiping his mouth with his sleeve and swaying. He leaned against a wall and took in some deep breaths of air.

"Never again what?" snapped Mollie, oblivious to what had happened after she distracted Dave away from Martha and Arthur. "What the hell's the matter with the two of you?"

"Wine," said Jumbo who by now had climbed out of the hedge. He brushed some leaves out of his hair and went to lean on a nearby window sill, missed it completely and fell over again.

As he struggled to his knees, he explained, "After the spooks disappeared, we 'ad to neck Martha and Arthur's wine quick before Dave saw the full glasses and asked a load of awkward questions. I'm OK with the odd beer but I've never had wine before and I'm buggered if I'll ever drink the f****** stuff again."

"That was one very close call, we was lucky, real lucky," slurred Bean, waving his finger at Mollie. He tried to follow his finger but failed. "You was quick, Mollie. You was bloody quick thinking distracting Dave about the till. You probably saved the day for Emma an' us an' the spooks an' I love you for that." He leaned on her and was promptly sick over the back of her hoodie.

"Get off me, you moron, this is my best hoodie. You two are proper pissed. You can't go home in this state 'cos Emma will get the blame. Come on, let's get you to my house and clean you up. You're both ratted!"

"I love yerr more than 'e does," said Jumbo, clumsily trying to put his arm around Mollie's shoulder.

"No, you don't," said Bean, pushing him off playfully.

"Yerr, I do. I really do."

Jumbo and Bean held onto Mollie for support and the three zigzagged off down the street, continuing their spat.

"No, you don't."

"I really do."

"Shut up the pair of you and try to walk straight or we'll all be falling over!"

# CHAPTER 13

Five weeks later the café was going great guns. Christmas was upon Emma before she turned around and *Crumpets* had broken its record turnover four months on the trot. November had been her best month ever.

The bypass had just started its rehousing phase and a sea of white vans jostled to park outside her café every morning. The queues for Emma's legendary bacon cobs were regularly out of the door and she now had to be up an hour earlier to be ready for the onslaught.

The banter in the café was lively, from the first ring of the doorbell of white-van-drivers in Santa hats until about 3.00 p.m. when worn-out mums, complete with loaded pushchairs arrived with tired angels and wise men straight from Bethlehem, all exhausted before the school Christmas holidays had even started! The mums just wanted to take the weight off their feet and for someone – anyone – to entertain the kids for a few moments.

At about 4.00 p.m. there was a short lull before either the book club, the knitting club, the W.I. committee or the local choir committee all came for coffee and cake on different days.

Mollie had become indispensable. She was there to open at 6.00 a.m. and often closed up at 6.00 p.m. despite both Dave and Emma trying to convince her to go home earlier. Dave no longer watched her every move at the till and she, in turn, had learned more and more from Emma about how to negotiate better deals from the suppliers. She also wanted to learn how to do the books and had ditched the nose ring on her own volition. She had become a diamond to *Crumpets*.

Dave had settled into café life and enjoyed the hustle and bustle. He had removed some unnecessary cost, much to Emma's delight, and they were secretly considering expanding by buying another café – *Crumpets 2*. They had already agreed that Mollie would be a key player if they did. As an alternative plan, Emma was all for the pair of them buying somewhere special to live as a true couple, but the current arrangement of two homes suited them both, for the time being. However, a decision would have to be made soon whether to invest in another café or to buy a house, they couldn't afford both.

To Emma's great delight, the spooks were still around. But after lengthy discussions between them and the hoodies, they all agreed it would be better for them to avoid all contact with Dave for the present time. Emma knew this decision would compound the difficulty she would face when the inevitable introductions finally came. How could she tell him, after all this time, that there were two spooks living at *Crumpets*, who had saved the café from total disaster several times? Why had she kept them a secret? She kept telling herself she hadn't told him because he wouldn't understand. He did reality and numbers, not spirits.

To avoid another episode with Dave arriving unexpectedly, Emma always waited until he had gone on one of his trips to Ireland before she invited everyone around. Arthur and Martha's company continued to be a delight and Emma had many riotous evenings with them and the three hoodies, although red wine was still taboo for Bean and Jumbo.

Upon turning sixteen, Jumbo, to his mother and father's delight, secured an apprenticeship with a local engineering company. However, Bean decided to stay on at school to get some more qualifications; he wanted to go to college to become a chef. Both scenarios pleased Emma no end. They were still regular visitors to *Crumpets*, although perhaps not quite so frequent because homework and girls were beginning to get in the way.

Next door, Dan had achieved his dream and bought the adjoining property to extend his butcher's shop. After much hassle he had convinced the council to agree to the change of use. He regularly called in the café, when they were both quiet, to tell Emma of his progress or seek her advice. He would excitedly spread his plans over the empty tables, genuinely wanting her help with colours and decor. He now had a shop twice the size, lived in a beautifully furnished flat above both and employed two lads as apprentices. His hours mirrored those of *Crumpets*. He was the biggest purchaser of bacon from suppliers in the county and Emma was his biggest customer.

Sadly, the newsagent had decided to retire, but sold his business to a delightful family who kept the shop open nearly eighteen hours a day.

Bucket Street was a happy street. *Crumpets* was the centre of everything, and Emma loved it.

Emma glanced up from the till late one afternoon and noticed a lone man sitting in one of the window seats and looking down the street. She hadn't seen or heard him come in, but that wasn't unusual for many times she had surfaced from the steamy kitchen only to find a completely empty or a completely rammed café. She was never surprised.

This customer was alone, and intriguing. She busied herself tidying the counter and watched him for a while. He picked up the local paper and when bored, put it down to just gaze out of the window and watch the world go by. The man had a considerably smarter appearance than her normal customers who were generally covered in tile glue or cement or had marks down the sides and tops of their overalls where hands had been idly wiped. The worst customers were the carpenters who left a trail of sawdust throughout her café.

This man could best be described as distinguished; fiftyish, well-built but bordering on under-exercised and slightly overfed. He had well-groomed hair, which was white at the back and sides and slightly darker on top. He wore a tweed jacket and when he turned around, Emma was surprised to see he was wearing a dog collar. A vicar in her café... this was unusual. In fact, she thought he was probably the first. A smartly dressed vicar who would turn heads and wasn't wearing a wedding ring was definitely a first. She could already hear the local, lonely women gossiping and exaggerating about the new heart-throb clergy frequenting the café. In turn, they would then start casually dropping into *Crumpets* in the hope of getting a glimpse of this man who would by then have been built up to be an available, middle-aged Adonis.

With this ploy in mind, Emma decided she needed to encourage him to come by regularly so went over to make him welcome. However, close up she realised he suffered from the scourge of many fifty-year-old men: hair sprouting from his nostrils and ears coupled with rampant dark eyebrows partially hidden behind dark, horn-rimmed ecclesiastical glasses. She also spotted three white hairs sprouting off-piste from the end of his nose, which had clearly escaped his notice for some time. Confirmation that he did not wear glasses when performing his shaving routine.

She was her normal cheerful self despite his professional uniform. During their initial meeting, she chuckled to herself deciding that the 'cougars' of Bucket Street and the surrounding area would soon have their tails up.

Those cougars who were young enough to see his defects were few and far between and would quickly make their own minds whether to hunt or avoid. The other even hungrier cougars, some of whom needed to focus through milk-bottle thick glasses, wouldn't care. In their imagination a pursuit and hopeful, 'kill' would be inevitable, courtesy of blue rinses, tighter corsets, balcony bras designed to return breasts to the centre, even breasts that had long since wandered East and West. These were just some of the rusty weapons that would again see the light of day from their dusty armoury. Clipped, affected accents would lure the innocent vicar and, in their dreams, they would soon be installed as his new wife.

Here's a man who has innocently swum into a pool of piranhas, thought Emma. He doesn't stand a chance!

However, this new customer could not have been more pleasant and Emma enjoyed their exchange. He introduced himself formally with a huge smile. "My name is Reverend Barnaby Clifton." Then added, "However, I am happy for folk to call me Vicar, the Vic or Barnaby. At the last parish they called me Rev because I rode on a moped!" He laughed out loud at his joke and Emma couldn't help but warm to him." He smiled more than any other vicar she had known. He continued, "I am taking over from the previous incumbent and I'm already looking forward to the challenges of the parish. I'll be moving into the old Vicarage shortly and will be looking for a cleaner as I live on my own." Then with mischief in his voice he asked, "I don't suppose you'd fancy the job?" He waited for her reply with a twinkle in his eye.

"What, me? Take on another job part-time? You must be joking! I haven't got time..." She was going to say 'to have a wee' but decided against it. "... to have my own lunch and I run a café!"

Barnaby laughed, countering with, "Well, you know the old saying, don't you?' If there aren't enough hours in the day, then steal some from the night!'"

"That's when I do my books and have my lunch." Emma laughed, enjoying the exchange.

"I jest. If you do think of someone suitable then please, I would be so grateful if you could put them in touch with me."

"Of course, I'll have a think and if you need anything else, you're only to ask," she said sincerely. Emma believed a long list of suitors, all claiming to be first-class cleaners, could fill *Crumpets* twice over if the vacancy was made public.

As the café was quiet, Emma made him a coffee and toasted him a teacake, on the house, as a welcome to the area.

Dave came over a little later and introduced himself and so did Mollie. Soon all four were chatting and laughing together around the bay window table. Emma decided Barnaby was going to be a welcome addition to the area, and especially *Crumpets*.

When Barnaby and Dave had gone, Emma and Mollie both came from different ends of the café at the same time, laughing helplessly. They both asked the question: "How on earth can we introduce Barnaby to Arthur and Martha?" Garlic necklaces and oak stakes entered into the conversation. It was a problem for another day they agreed. Still, neither could concentrate as they locked up the café for the night, amid bursts of laughter imagining Arthur offering Barnaby a pinch of snuff.

# CHAPTER 14

"I can't thank you enough for telling me about the job opportunity at the vicarage," whispered Lillian when she popped back into the café just before closing on a quiet Monday with a bunch of flowers for Emma. "I had an interview this afternoon with the new vicar and he offered me the job right there and then! I couldn't believe it. It's more money than working in the council's planning office and he said we can talk about my hours to suit my boys. And when he heard I was once a hotel cook, well, he was over the moon."

"I'm so, so pleased for you. It wasn't necessary to bring flowers, but it was very kind and they are beautiful," said Emma.

"He's such a lovely man and so courteous," continued Lillian, waving away Emma's thanks. "He quietly shared with me that he doubted the other two candidates, who he had already interviewed, knew a feather duster from a ladle, and would probably have had to stop for a breather on the way up to the second floor. He was lovely to talk to and I felt I could work for this man, there and then."

Lillian's excitement continued as she recounted other things he shared with her. Emma smiled at her enthusiasm. "He also said," Lillian continued, "that he nearly passed out in the other interviews, intoxicated by industrial strength cologne and tombola perfume. He wondered if they had swum in it before coming in. So much for spraying it in the air, waiting a few seconds and then walking through the mist. He thought they probably misunderstood the concept and did it the wrong way around!" Lillian laughed. "I think that was a compliment to me, but I'm not sure. Anyway, we had a giggle about it."

"So, what are your duties?" asked Emma. "Tell me all about it." She was excited for Lillian and keen to know more.

"Mainly cleaning; making sure his bedroom, study, entrance hall, stairs and kitchen are sparkling. Whoever cleaned before was quite thorough. I think it must have been the previous vicar's wife. He asked if I would cook a full English breakfast for him on the mornings I'm in early and 'some good wholesome pies and puddings' when he occasionally has friends and local dignitaries around for dinner. I agreed then he said the job was mine. Of course, I said, 'no problem'. I can't thank you enough, Emma. I'm so lucky." She patted Emma's arm in gratitude.

"I'm delighted you secured the position. I'm sure you'll be happy there. You deserve a bit of excitement in your life having worked for the council all this time, it will be so different," said Emma, smiling and meaning every word.

———

Three weeks later Lillian called into *Crumpets* again to let Emma know how things were going. She was still very excited about the job and explained she was deep cleaning each room, starting at the front door. Lillian explained the vicar had now fully moved in and she had cooked him a full English breakfast on three mornings.

"He likes black-pudding – ughh!" She pretended to put one finger down her throat before continuing, "As well as sausages, bacon, eggs, mushrooms and lots of hot, white toast and thick cut marmalade afterwards. And goodness only knows where he puts all the coffee he drinks."

Emma added, "I love it when a man really enjoys what I cook for them. It makes me feel appreciated."

"I agree," replied Lillian. " But he can really put it away. I think he could eat one more hash-brown than a pig!" Emma was shocked at the expression and laughed out loud.

Lillan carried on describing her new role, "I'm surprised he doesn't seem to have much furniture of his own, but the departing couple had downsized and generously left him some to be going on with. He also gave me a wad of money to buy sheets and towels with, and to fill up the larder and wine stocks. There must have been at least £300 in the envelope, Emma. I was shocked he trusted me so early on in the job but I was absolutely in heaven – a shopping spree with someone else's money! Of course, I bought the best and meticulously kept all the receipts, but he wasn't interested in the cost at all. Trusted me implicitly!"

Emma gave her a little squeeze. "You're clearly going to be brilliant at the job. He's very lucky to have you, Lillian. It sounds as though you're more of a housekeeper than a cleaner."

Lillian nodded, pride evident on her face. "He's asked if I'll cook for some of his friends in a couple of weeks' time. I'm a bit nervous as I haven't done anything fancy for a while. He said he would leave the menu to me, perhaps you could help me put some ideas together?"

"Of course, I will. It'll be fun working with you and if you need some help with serving the first dinner, I'll be there."

"He also said he was a keen gardener. He has heaps and heaps of magazines about garden layouts stacked everywhere and said he'll get someone in to reorganise the vicarage garden, especially the overgrown area where the previous vicar let it grow wild. He shared with me that he's always wanted a nine-foot-tall stone pillar located in a secret area of the garden. He described to me where he wants it, which he thinks would be the perfect spot. However, I'm not so sure. If I remember correctly from when I was a little girl, it's where the old vicar buried all his pet dogs, cats, budgies and even a parrot," nattered on Lillian.

"What? The old vicar had a parrot?" exclaimed Emma.

"Yes, a big, evil, green and red parrot. The place the new vicar has chosen will be a proper boneyard because the old vicar took in every stray cat and dog in the parish. Whenever a parishioner died and left a pet, the vicar took them in, including the parrot. Then, when any of the orphaned pets died, he buried them in his wild garden."

Lillian paused for breath briefly, then continued. Emma smiled inside for her new friend.

"I used to go to the vicarage with the Sunday school and we were all frightened of the parrot. Nasty thing it was. It would take your finger off at the knuckle if you weren't careful. The vicar was forever conducting services with bandaged fingers. He called it Stroganoff and threatened if it bit him one more time it would become a new dish... Polly Stroganoff!" Emma laughed.

"The place the new vicar has chosen for his stone pillar is right at the end of the garden, and out of sight of the road and all the neighbours, he thinks it will be ideal. He wants it all sorted before his friends come for dinner in a couple of weeks and surprise them! I think that if he can get anyone around here to do any building work in a couple of weeks, he will surprise us all!" Lillian smiled at the memory of his naivety. "He'll certainly have to pull some strings. Mind you, he should have some pretty good connections, him being a vicar and all that, don't you think?" She tapped her nose and knowingly pointed upwards.

"You're enjoying the job already, aren't you?" asked Emma, loving Lilian's obvious enthusiasm and energy.

"Yes, I am, but I've decided to be a bit careful or I'll end up doing everything. I'll sort out the cooking and cleaning, but I'm keeping well clear of the garden. If I'm not careful, he'll have me tending the borders before I cook breakfast and probably push a broom up my bum to sweep the paths while I'm cutting the grass!"

Emma burst out laughing at the image. "You're terrible, Lillian!"

———

To be fair to Barnaby Clifton, like all his ideas, by the time he was ready to tell folk what he had in mind he had already set things in motion. Within days of informing Lillian of his landscape plans, a yellow digger was trundling down his garden path early in the morning on its way to the pet cemetery.

Two days later, the wild garden had been flattened and a new area of lawn laid. One day after that the standing stone pillar had been erected and was surrounded by a paved area of grey slabs. To offer further screening, a tall mature hedge of beech and leylandii had been planted surrounding the paved area. That part of the garden was transformed.

Lillian relayed to Emma, with a blush, that the vicar had winked at her when he told her that he always made more progress by seeking forgiveness rather than permission.

"My job," she told Emma, "while all this had been happening, was to provide teas and coffees and sandwiches for the workmen, whom can best be described as the Chinese army marching down the garden at 7.30 a.m. and back at 5.00 p.m. with only a short break at midday. They never stopped; they were amazing. And they all seemed cheerful, whizzing their wheelbarrows up the garden with fresh soil and sand, and wheeling rubbish back to their lorries in the drive. I've never seen anything like it in my life." Lillian shook her head in disbelief at what she had witnessed. "The new vicar was there at the start of the working day and he was the last to finish. At mid-morning on Friday, he called everyone together near the house and out he went with a mountain of bacon cobs and gallons of hot coffee. You can guess who had been making them for the previous hour, can't you? Muggins here." Lillian pointed at her head. "Moi."

"Wow," said Emma, thinking Lillian never stopped either.

Lillian continued, "For the rest of the day it was as if the whole team had been super-charged. They were nearly running. It was just incredible. Just because of a bacon cob!" Lillian shook her head in amazement and then whispered to

Emma, "I wondered if he had put something in the bacon when I wasn't looking!"

They both chuckled mischievously.

# CHAPTER 15

"Any colour: yellow, red, pink, scarlet, green or orange. Just not blue. Please don't be blue," Emma said out loud. "Please, please, please, please, not blue. Not yet."

Emma went for a shower to pass the time as she waited the ten minutes to see if her life was about to change for ever. However, only a few moments passed before she emerged from her tiny shower; her tiny shower that was shoe-horned into her minuscule bathroom, in her rabbit hutch flat. Normally, she would take a twenty-minute shower in the evening in order to wash away the café's stains and smells and then a quick shower in the morning to mentally arrange her to-do list and psych herself up for the coming day. But not today.

Her mind was in turmoil. A baby would change all her plans. She wasn't ready, not yet. She had talked casually about the prospect of a baby with Dave a few times, but there wasn't any real commitment from him. There had been flippant chats about a baby pink or blue bedroom, but nothing serious. He usually closed the conversation down whenever she joked about it. She thought it was because he was a bit scared and so they'd never had a real, concrete discussion about boundaries, responsibilities and how life would change for them both.

Why is that? She wondered to herself. Why haven't we ever had that discussion? Don't I love him? Isn't he the best lover I have ever been with? Doesn't he have prospects? Is there someone else?

Yes, she did love him. Yes, he could be fantastic in bed although she hadn't had many others with whom to compare. Yes, he could walk into an accountancy job anywhere. No, she didn't believe there was anyone else.

So, what was the problem?

The flat doorbell rang and rang urgently and Mollie called up the stairs for Emma to shake herself. "There's money to be made and bacon to be cooked and white-van-drivers are beginning to jostle for parking spaces outside, bumper-to-bumper already."

# CHAPTER 16

Barnaby Clifton became an instant hit in the parish. Over the next three months his inherited congregation flourished from, perhaps eight elderly parishioners on a dry, sunny Sunday morning to about forty parishioners of all ages.

Each Sunday now, regardless of the unpredictable spring weather, his church was filling up with newcomers and those who had been absent since their own christenings. His services were light and infectious, peppered with humour and inclusive of children and pensioners alike. He had a wealth of anecdotes to complement his services and used a range of outrageous props to make his sermons come to life.

He quickly became booked up for weddings for the foreseeable future, and mixed the right amount of solemnity for the occasion with the opportunity to celebrate the future of the happy couple.

For funerals, Barnaby spent many hours researching those who had passed away and often received comments such as: "You spoke as though you really knew my mum."

He had a winning way with both the elderly women parishioners and the male parishioners. He gripped the hands of the men firmly and shook them with vigour. No wet lettuce leaf, wishy-washy, limp, ecumenical greeting from Barnaby Clifton; he knew they didn't like that. He held both of the hands of the elderly women gently with both of his, smiled and looked into their eyes as he spoke to them.

The Mother's Union frequently invited him to their meetings, which he never left without loading his bicycle saddlebag with homemade cakes.

As a result of an increased congregation, the Sunday school expanded exponentially and suddenly there was no shortage of willing, young mums to help.

Lillian fell under his spell too, offering to do more for him and the vicarage, despite her early misgivings. She shopped for him, cooked and cleaned for him, and when he had a dinner with friends, she found herself waiting on his table for him. Occasionally, she stopped and shook her head wondering how all these extra duties had crept up on her, but such was the magnetism of Barnaby Clifton.

Inevitably, a small clique of ancient parishioners was less than welcoming towards the new vicar and his plethora of 'new-fangled nonsense' as they called it. They missed the pedestrian, predictable pace of the last vicar, but they were in the minority and quickly overruled when lamenting the departure of the last vicar and his wife. Barnaby dismissed their criticisms and when he spoke to Lillian he referred to them, in a derogatory tone as: "The small brigade of parishioners who play dominoes and smell of mothballs."

The first ever parish youth club was set up under his stewardship and, although it grew slowly, it did grow and eventually twenty youngsters were off street corners and children's playgrounds and letting off steam in the village hall every Friday night. Barnaby occasionally called in and, to the youngsters' delight, he played a passable game of Killer with the dart players, saw off a few frames with the billiard players, giving tips to his competitors, and with his jacket off, he could keep up and jive with the best of them. Most importantly, he encouraged the wallflowers to get up and have a go.

The youngsters concluded he was one cool vicar.

His next challenge was to instigate a parish magazine. Now, a parish magazine requires a clever skillset not readily available in most parishes, which initially caused him to scratch his head.

The dominoes and mothballs brigade delighted in the difficulties and delays Barnaby was facing, smugly wondering if he had bitten off more than he could chew with the project. They were secretly looking forward to watching Barnaby Clifton having to admit defeat.

However, Barnaby Clifton was too streetwise a cat to be stuffed by grumpy old naysayers and he set out to do what he did best. He combined the imaginative skills of some of the creative youth club youngsters who attended the local well respected art school with the organisational capabilities of one of his parishioners – a Mrs Nancy Bains.

Nancy had been a bank manager's secretary but now she was recently retired and desperately looking for a new challenge in life. Despite having worked in such a dusty, staid profession for so many years she had bounce and enthusiasm. She was a breath of fresh air to Barnaby and an answer to his prayer.

Nancy's husband worked away for most of the week so she was flattered by the vicar's approach and jumped at the opportunity of a project working with youngsters... and the new vicar! Barnaby and Nancy met regularly on a weekday evening at her house, creating a magazine that would have been welcome in parishes of a much larger size. Not only did they create the document, but they organised teams of parishioners to collect articles for inclusion, collate the material, print the magazine, construct the booklet and distribute it to every house in the parish. It was paid for local business advertisements. *Crumpets* was one of the first to take a full-page spread.

Emma was keen to support the vicar for he often had his church meetings in *Crumpets* and coffee and cake were always part of the agenda. Some attendees even succumbed to two slices of cake following Barnaby's lead. He knew how to seduce a committee into starting promptly, willingly agreeing to commit to achieving objectives before the next meeting, and excitedly contributing throughout the meeting while also having fun.

Examples of the sort of style the new parish magazine front cover should take were sought and circulated for voting. Their content ranged from downright irreligious to such stunning artwork it could well grace a city church's magazine. The parish voted upon all the entries and there was an outright winner – a lad from the youth club. So, as a treat, the whole youth club was treated to a fish and chip supper. There were nearly twice the number of members that night. Funny that!

The village quidnuncs grossly exaggerated their insidious whisperings about the amount of time Barnaby and Nancy were spending together. Other disparagements from the dominoes and mothball brigade included criticisms about the shortness of Barnaby's Sunday services, the youths tumbling noisily out of the youth club on Friday nights, and the congestion created by the parked pushchairs blocking the pavement outside the very successful mother and toddler mornings. Barnaby dismissed them with a wave of his hand.

"When good things are being created, there are always those who don't have a clue where to start on such projects and wouldn't know how to build such a winning team, but openly criticize and kick the new sandcastles down rather than acknowledge any achievement," he explained to Nancy. "Every parish has such a brigade; the skill is learning how to circumnavigate them."

The first edition of the parish magazine was a huge success. Just one day after the first edition was launched, all of the second edition's advertising space was sold out and a party was held in the vicarage to mark the occasion.

Nancy and Barnaby continued to have their meetings at her house. Incidentally, the coffee at Nancy's house had imperceptibly morphed into red wine and the biscuits had innocently morphed into supper. They worked well together and Nancy enjoyed the responsibility of the project. Barnaby was fun to work with and they laughed a lot.

However, after a particularly late finish one Wednesday evening, as Barnaby switched on his bicycle lights and climbed onto the saddle, he noticed at least three late night dog walkers murmuring in a huddle and looking his way. He wondered if they had been staking the house out in relays. A letter from the bishop would soon follow in response to the inevitable, anonymous complaint.

Barnaby shook his head as he cycled home that balmy evening. "I only wish I was having as much fun as they all think I am," he said to himself.

# CHAPTER 17

For the past three months, Emma had stopped taking the pregnancy tests. She didn't know what outcome she wanted and flitted from one end of the colour spectrum to the other. She had thrown the unused tests away and decided to let nature take its course. Whatever happened, she would live with it.

And so life carried on at *Crumpets*.

The noisy white-van-drivers jostled in every morning, the weary mums arrived in the early afternoon and the peaceful clubs of mainly elderly customers concluded the days.

One evening, Lillian called in to *Crumpets* to see Emma after closing time and it was obvious something was troubling her. Her normal jovial manner was missing and furrows were etched across her forehead. Lillian was in a real fret.

Emma sensed the change immediately and silently placed a cup of coffee in front of her, along with a plate of chocolate biscuits. Lillian didn't immediately take one, which was another sign that things weren't right. After a few minutes, Emma broke the silence and asked, "Well?"

"It's Barnaby." Lillian sniffed, taking a few sips of her drink.

"What about him? He was in here today, his usual larger than life self, with an entourage of young mums dribbling all over him. They all had their hands in the air saying, 'Pick me, pick me, pick me to run the event.' And that was just a Bring and Buy sale in the church hall," said Emma.

"He's lovely, but something is wrong and I don't know what it is. Well, I think I do, but I can't even say it to myself," said Lillian. "He's such a complex man."

A million scenarios began shooting through Emma's head. Had Barnaby made a pass at Lillian? Had he committed some terrible crime she's just found out about? Were there skeletons in his cupboard? Was he a fraud and not a real vicar? She decided to let Lillian tell her in her own time. By now they had finished their drinks. Another coffee was due.

After making them, Emma sat back down opposite Lillian.

"It wasn't until I started to think of things that were happening, or had already happened, that it all started to fall into place," Lillian began.

"What started to fall into place? What has he done? You aren't making any sense. He hasn't hit you, has he? Or worse?" Emma put her hand on Lillian's arm to show she was not alone.

"No! No, it's nothing like that... " Lillian paused while she tried to put things in order in her own mind.

Emma struggled but stayed silent, drinking her coffee. She decided this was serious.

"You know I told you I have always gone to church, even as a little girl? Well, some things were drummed into me from a very early age, and when you are young you don't really understand, do you? Well, what it all meant is beginning to unfold in front of my eyes and it's very scary. You're going to think me very silly, Emma."

"Let me be the judge of that, shall we? Now, what's Barnaby done that is so awful?"

There was another long pause as Lillian wondered how to start. She picked up her cup then put it straight back down again. "Do you remember me telling you that he was erecting a huge stone pillar in the old vicar's wild garden. Well, Barnaby goes there every morning, kneels down and prays to it."

"You mean he goes to his quiet place to pray, not he prays to it?"

"No, he prays to it! In a strange language! I arrived very early one morning because my youngest lad was doing something special in the school assembly and I wanted to watch him. I thought I'd get to the vicarage really early, get on top of my work and then return to finish off later. That's when I heard it. I couldn't believe it."

"You heard what?"

"Up in the garden. Chanting. Very quietly, like. Weird it was. I walked very carefully on the grass so as not to disturb him. It was definitely him, I'm sure. I wondered if he was 'speaking in tongues'. It unnerved me, I can tell you, so I crept back to the vicarage. I couldn't concentrate on my work so I went to the assembly which, by the way, was lovely with all the kids together singing. My youngest had a speaking part; I was so proud of him. But my mind kept wandering back to the vicarage garden. When I arrived back, there was Barnaby, as normal, asking if I had time to knock him up some toast and marmalade as though nothing had happened."

"What's speaking in tongues? I don't understand. We all use our tongues to speak, don't we?" asked a completely confused Emma.

"No, speaking in tongues is when a person is experiencing an intense religious state, an ecstasy, a sort of trance. They utter a string of incomprehensible sounds, which normally need interpreting by someone else. But I didn't see anyone else there. It's a way some religions communicate with their Gods. It's used in Haitian voodoo ceremonies, African and Asian shamanic religions, and Alaskan native religions."

"I think I'm beginning to get the picture now and understand why you are so upset. But how do you know all this?" asked a wide-eyed Emma.

"My gran had the gift of speaking in tongues and took me along to her church once. I didn't understand a thing. I was quite frightened by the experience. My mum went nuts when she found out."

"I can imagine why you were so frightened," reassured Emma. "How old were you?"

"About six. That's not all. I heard him having a right royal argument with his father on the phone today. He said his mother was, 'as nutty as a fruit cake and should be in a home'. It was an awful row. Now do you see why I'm so worried? He ended up shouting, 'God almighty, Dad, what have I got to do to make you see sense? Get her into a home before she sets fire to the bloody place!'"

"I'm sorry, but I'm not entirely following you, Lillian. Let me run through this again. Barnaby prays in the garden and had a row with his dad. So? Loads of people go to their special places and pray, although not necessarily in an ecstatic trance like voodoo, I grant you. And I can't count the number of times I've fallen out with my mum and dad."

Lillian shook her head with exasperation.

"Don't you see, Emma? Have I got to spell it out to you? He's erected a graven image in the garden and he prays to it! He shouldn't take God's name in vain but he shouted 'God Almighty' at the top of his voice on the phone. He shouldn't talk to either of his parents in such a derogatory manner because he should honour his mother and father. Do you understand now why I'm concerned?"

Emma nodded as understanding slowly began to dawn. "I'm right with you Lillian... I think."

"Let me go on."

"There's more?"

"Lots. Next, he shouldn't bear false witness."

"What on earth does that mean, for goodness sake?" queried Emma.

"It means he shouldn't lie!"

"When did Barnaby lie? I've never heard him lie about anything."

"I'll tell you exactly when. He should have sought written permission from the bishop to change the layout of the vicarage garden before he built things in it like his big stone pillar. And do you know what he said? Shall I tell you? You won't believe me, but I will anyway. He said he would get the bishop pissed on claret over lunch, take him for a walk around the garden if he can still stand, and if he questions the layout, he would tell him it was always like that! An outright lie. Outright deception. Can you believe it? It keeps me awake just thinking about it."

Emma shrugged. "It's not really a lie, is it? It's more of a porky pie than an outright lie," she said, in Barnaby's defence.

"How can you say that? He's a man of God and should set an example in everything he does!"

"I think you're being a bit harsh, Lillian."

"OK then, what about not coveting his neighbour's wife, male or female servant, ox or donkey? He's around at Nancy Bains's house more often than the milkman! And only on weekday evenings when her husband's away. His bike knows its own way there now and is chained up outside her house till all hours of the night. The whole congregation is talking about them."

Emma finished her coffee, digesting the information.

Then, again, she tried to defend the man she had come to call a friend. "Surely, the only way the whole congregation would know about this is if some malicious person told them? Maybe it's the... what does Barnaby call them? The bingo and peppermint brigade or something like that. The folk who want him out and the old vicar, who we used to call Rigour Mortice, back in. And what's all this about Nancy having an ox or a donkey? As far as I know she has no pets at all, not even a goldfish. And as for a male or female servant, I think she only has a cleaner two mornings a week? It doesn't make any sense."

Ignoring Emma's counter arguments, Lillian continued. "Finally, he of all people should keep the sabbath holy, shouldn't he? And that's the day he has the dinners for all his boozy friends. I should know – I cook and the next morning I take all the bottles to the recycling. It's often a full car load. I'm there for ages. Folk stop to watch me. It's so embarrassing, they must think I have an alcohol problem!" Lillian put her head in her hands. Nearly shouting, she said, "All this and he's supposed to be a bloody vicar!"

Emma didn't even bother to try to reply this time. She thought it best to just let Lillian get it all out of her system.

"You know the only two commandments he hasn't broken yet, don't you, Emma?" asked Lillian quietly a couple of minutes later, finally calmer.

"Well, yes, but just remind me of them," mumbled Emma, trying to keep up.

"Thou shall not commit adultery and thou shalt not kill. How long will it be before he ticks them off too? And I'm in the middle of all this doing all the cleaning and opening up the vicarage before he's even out of bed!"

"I see," said Emma very quietly, although she didn't really. But she understood this was very serious stuff to Lillian. She gave her a big hug and suggested she go home, not talk to anyone else about it and they could talk again in two days' time.

# CHAPTER 18

Emma felt unnerved by what Lillian had told her about Barnaby and couldn't wait for Arthur and Martha to arrive that evening to share her concerns. As soon as they came through the door, she locked it behind them and unloaded all her worries before they even had chance to sit down.

The calmer of the two of them, Martha, spoke first. "Emma, first of all, we are gasping for a cup of tea and Arthur is famished, as always. So, he will make the tea and you and I will sit down, and you can tell me all about it again slowly, if that's OK with you?"

"Sorry, yes, it all came out in a bit of a rush, didn't it? Right, I'll start again. You both know of Lillian, Jumbo's mum?" asked Emma.

They both nodded, Martha from her seat in front of Emma and Arthur from behind the counter.

"Well, she was successful in getting the cleaning job at the vicarage. You've not met Barnaby, the new vicar, yet as I've no idea how to introduce you. What with you being spirits and all that and him being a man of the cloth, I didn't want him coming around here thinking he was doing me a favour by trying to exorcise you."

Martha smiled.

"Well, back to Lillian. Everything's gone very well for her and she has been thoroughly enjoying working for him. She's been there for about three months now. However, she came to see me earlier here in the café after closing and was in a dreadful state."

Arthur returned to the table with cups and a pot of tea, and he and Martha sat patiently waiting for whatever was so dreadful, silently imagining all sorts of things.

"Well, she thinks he's a fraud, a complete charlatan. And in her mind, she has proof!"

"What kind of proof is that then, my dear?" asked Martha thoughtfully.

"Well, he's put up a big stone pillar in his garden and chants or prays to it every morning."

Arthur asked a question, "Prays *to* it, or goes there to pray?"

"Aha, exactly what I said!" replied Emma, delighted someone else had spotted the difference too. "You think just like me, Arthur. But Lillian was adamant that he kneels down and chants or prays to it using his tongue, I think she said."

"Most interesting." Arthur pondered and poured the teas. "I think you mean he was speaking in tongues. It's called glossolalia. Anything else?"

"He shouts at his father on the phone and wants to put his mother in a home. He swears and blasphemes. He told Lillian he will get the bishop pissed and lie about what he has done in the garden, telling him it was always like it. And he spends loads of time in Nancy Bains's house till late at night when her husband is away."

Arthur looked at Martha, a knowing look that suggested that although all this seemed quite serious, he was struggling to follow. Martha inferred this and returned the look.

"Is there anything else?" queried Arthur.

"Yes." Emma nodded. "Lillian thinks the only two commandments he hasn't broken are 'thou shalt not commit adultery' and 'thou shalt not kill'. She's right in the middle of all this and she's worried about how long it will be before he ticks those two off too. So, what do you think?" She glanced between Arthur and Martha, hoping for an explanation or some insight.

"What do we think about what?" A confused Arthur shook his head.

"Well, is she safe?" Emma asked, holding her hands up and shrugging.

"He's a vicar, a man of the cloth, my dear. I'm sure she's safe," replied a bewildered Martha, wondering why anyone would ask such a question. However, seeing how concerned Emma was, she moderated her tone, "We can see you are worried sick. Would you like us to look into it?" she asked.

"Oh, please, will you? I'm so worried about Lillian. I think she will do something silly like confront him or report him to the bishop or de-frock him or whatever is the right word." Emma jumped up and hugged them both.

"Confronting him may not be such a bad thing. It may simply explain everything," replied Arthur thoughtfully.

After a few moments of reflection Emma said, "*Crumpets* is getting a reputation as a place to bring problems. I will soon be competing with Barnaby as an agony aunt."

"You should be flattered that people feel safe here and trust you," reassured Martha.

# CHAPTER 19

Barnaby's days in the community were packed full. He spent his time tending to the spiritual needs of his congregation and offering solace to those in need. Christenings, funerals, fetes, ecumenical meetings, church choir practice and school visits were also squashed into what was left of his days. He felt he was working eight days a week.

Outwardly, he presented an unyielding dedication to every member of his congregation: always available, always had time, never rushed, always on call, always caring. However, secretly, his subconscious was willing the hours in the day to speed by and for it be evening. The evening then needed to morph quickly into the dark of night when he could jump on his old bicycle and head for Nancy's house on 'parish magazine business'. This was the time when the fewest members of the dominoes and mothball brigade would be out dog walking or nosing about in other peoples' business.

Barnaby struggled with his conscience on two counts. Firstly, he struggled with this new set of all consuming emotions which were taking on a seriousness of their own. Secondly, he struggled with his duty to remain faithful to his calling and his congregation. He had to admit, when he was being honest with himself in quiet times, that in the battle for his attention, the more earthly calling was winning, hands down. It worried him greatly. The one saving grace seemed to be that Nancy's husband was spending more and more time working away. Her husband now regularly stayed away at the weekends as well as week days and Nancy valued Barnaby's company.

Once the first parish magazine had been published, Barnaby's reasons for meeting with Nancy in the evenings were dwindling. The magazine had become a huge success with an amazing following in the parish. Advertisers were flocking to be seen in it. The vicar's address at the front was the first page readers turned to, for he mentioned parishioners by name and the good work they were doing. Not just the great and the good of the parish, but the litter pickers, the church's volunteer grass cutting team and the regular visitors of the sick. This just spurred them all on to even greater achievements.

A monthly management meeting would be all that was necessary to ensure the magazine's continued momentum for the future. Barnaby's realisation that he would have to wait three weeks to see Nancy was appalling to him, not meeting more regularly kept him awake.

He had so looked forward to that time in the evening, when the business of the magazine was done and they could engage in conversations about life, philosophy and human experience. It was a joy for him to spend time with her. She had an infectious laugh, was positive about life and the future, could think deeply, challenged him, was fun and... she was very attractive. Anticipation about their forthcoming meetings and what might be the outcome consumed his subconscious every waking hour and reflections on their recent deep conversations interfered with his sleep. He wondered if hidden meanings had been peppered in her conversation and whether, in his excitement, perhaps he had missed them.

Barnaby found himself teetering on the brink of temptation and he had only been in the parish for six months.

Then, on the most memorable evening of all, when all conversation was exhausted between them, wine glasses had been refilled and supper dishes cleared, a silence painted the room with, *tonight is different,* colours. The atmosphere between them changed. It was urgent, charged, as though there was an unfamiliar excitement and both hearts had moved up a gear trying to read each other's next move. Candlelight from a dozen flickering candles explored the corners of the room and wove their magic. Barnaby couldn't remember feeling like this for decades.

At his suggestion, they stood up from comfy chairs to face each other, moving closer in an excuse to chink glasses and toast the success of the magazine. Now near enough to look into her eyes, he was mesmerised by the almond flecks of colour in her iris that he had never seen before.

In turn, her eyes were searching his face, the crow's feet, the dimple in his chin, his unfathomable eyes in the silence between them, wondering how he would react to being kissed. How he would kiss her back? Would he be tender and gentle or would the kiss be an explosion of passion mixed with guilt? Nancy was searching for reassurance.

Suddenly, it seemed as though their minds were finally made up. It would be tonight. It would happen here and now. All their separate dreams, which had run along parallel tracks so far, had come together tonight, driven by an urgent urge to hold, to be held. The orange glow of the candles shepherded them together.

Moving imperceptibly closer, Nancy touched his bare arm which sent her feelings spiralling out of control. Her breathing mirrored her heartbeat. Barnaby felt goosebumps creep over his bare arms, he could hardly breath. Nancy started to close her eyes and turn her mouth to connect with his when...

Darkness. Blackness. Unexpected. Sudden.

In the closed-curtained room, all the candles had been unnervingly extinguished in one go, by an unexplained puff of wind. Nancy held onto Barnaby's arm tightly in the dark, frightened by the change. They were statues.

Not a candle was left alight. The darkness was complete. A darkness that could be felt, but not touched.

As quickly as they had been extinguished, all the candles in the room incomprehensibly flared alight again.

Barnaby and Nancy quickly moved apart, embarrassed by their closeness, both hit by the same realisation that they had been about to cross a line that could never be uncrossed. Flustered and puzzled, both mumbled apologies and received reassurances from each other that it was not their fault.

Barnaby hurriedly left.

# CHAPTER 20

Exactly three months after the previous test, again the line wasn't blue. "Thank goodness for that," Emma said stoically to herself.

Despite throwing away the unused tests, three months ago, she had changed her mind and bought some more. She suggested to herself that it would be prudent to have some in the flat on a just-in-case basis. Now her life could stay on the same trajectory since she first opened *Crumpets* nearly two years ago. She could continue to embrace the café with open arms. She could plan growth in her venture in the form of *Crumpets 2* or a new home. The realisation of the enormity of the changes had the test been positive startled her. The release felt like freedom.

Emma breathed a sigh of relief and... immediately burst into tears. Big tears, tears from deep, deep down. Tears of disappointment shook her body to the core. She dismissed the fact that, not two minutes ago, she had been praying for the line to be any colour other than blue. She blinked back tears trying to compose herself, and failed. The tears flowed and flowed and flowed.

It should have been blue, thought Emma. Deep down she had really wanted it to be blue. She didn't know why, but right now, it should have been blue. Deep blue. The deep blue of positivity. She wanted it to have been blue more than anything else in the world.

Emma now understood what it was like to yearn for what might have been. What could have been. What should have been. She was angry. It wasn't fair. It was her turn to make the leap from woman to motherhood. She was ready. She was sure she was ready. No, she wasn't sure at all that she was ready but, in the seconds since she had seen the negative test result, the thought of being pregnant had taken root in her mind. Right now, Emma desperately wanted a baby of her own.

Pangs of sadness suddenly weighed her down. Boys and girls' names she had subconsciously whispered out loud in the loneliness of the night came flooding back to her. She recalled distant dreams of cuddling her baby and singing lullabies from her lowest level of awareness, never allowing them to surface in the morning light.

Would the yearning pass? Not the way she was feeling right now.

The universe had its own plans and timings for Emma and these did not coincide with her current confused desires. In life's uncertainties, disappointment lingers long, but Emma was not to understand this concept just now. However, her innate determination to believe in herself and even the very low odds of success, would define the next chapters of her life. The balance between her short-term selfish desire to retain her status quo unencumbered by a baby and the emptiness of the rest of her life had just been tilted by providence.

Despite the long working hours, the café gave her and Dave a comfortable income and independence. Just occasionally, they had snatched a night away and enjoyed the guiltiness of their escape. She wanted those times to continue. How would that work in the future with a baby? It would shatter the tranquil balance they enjoyed. Their world would never be the same again.

Several of her friends, now young mums, talked endlessly about babies, how they had decorated the nursery, what had been baby's first words, and nappies.

"Goodness!" she had exclaimed as discussions about nappies covered contents, shapes, performance and even what oozed out in the nights. She and Dave had secretly criticized the new limited conversations of their friends, but her thoughts had now diametrically swung one hundred and eighty degrees. These were conversations Emma now wanted to join in with. She wanted to share her experiences of her own baby with her friends.

Emma knew that convincing herself of a wonderfully, completely new, topsy-turvy life was fairy land and it would not be quite so straightforward. She needed to protect herself from the crushing sadness of negative results. She would need to train herself to be stoic. But the day would come, she knew it. Her day, when the line would be the right colour and life would be turned upside down.

In Emma's new mindset, she wanted to wake one magical morning, tip toe into the bathroom and whisper a silent prayer. Then bounce back into the bedroom, jump on the bed and watch her partner's eyes light up when she told him the news. She wanted him to share in the joy and work with her to become amazing parents stumbling into the beautiful chaos of parenthood.

Slowly she gathered herself and made her way downstairs from her flat, only to burst into tears again when she saw Mollie, who threw her arms around her and pleaded to know what was wrong.

In the absence of any explanation, Mollie bustled Emma back upstairs and closed her door. Emma lay back on her bed and sobbed.

———

Mollie's competent hands then flew around the kitchen at one hundred miles per hour as there were normally two of them doing the cooking together.

"Where's the gaffer?" shouted the first white-van-driver in the queue.

"Emigrated! Couldn't face you another day!" replied Mollie from the kitchen to laughter from the queue.

"But I brighten her day, don't I, lads? I brighten everybody's day, don't I?"

More guffaws of laughter and banter flew back and forward.

"I'm cut to the core by your comment," shouted the first white-van-driver to Mollie.

"You should be," came the chorus from the queue. "We'd all emigrate from you if we could."

The banter only stopped when Mollie brought out the first four mega breakfasts.

An hour later, when the initial rush had diminished, Emma came downstairs with red raw eyes and began to help in the kitchen.

Mollie knew not to question her, but let Emma compose herself for when she might be ready to talk. Emma lasted just an hour and returned to her flat for the rest of the day. Fortunately, the café was unusually quiet, it being the November half-term school holiday.

Emma couldn't face the thought of people and stayed in her flat until nearly closing time. She apologised to Mollie when she came back down and busied herself polishing the counter. She was cleaning it for the third time and was about to start on it again when Mollie stopped her. She gently put her hand on Emma's arm.

"Perhaps you could clean the tables and chairs 'cos we'll need to re-varnish the counter if you clean it again." She smiled then asked, "What's wrong, Emma?"

Emma put her head on her arms on top the counter and sobbed. Mollie rubbed her back not knowing what to do when Barnaby put his arm around Emma's shoulders and led her to a table near the window. He sat her down and turned the sign on the door to closed.

"Two pots of tea and two toasted teacakes with lashings of butter please, Mollie," he said.

Mollie returned to the counter, grateful for the arrival of the cavalry.

"Whenever I am feeling sad, I find eating helps. It's comfort food, I suppose. By the size of my tummy, you can deduce that I'm often sad." With that, Barnaby put his head on one side and made a sad face. "Chips are an amazing antidote to sadness, especially with gravy, but the very best cure in the whole world a large tin of hot baked beans on two slices of wholemeal toast oozing butter. And if one is really sad, it should be sprinkled with grated cheese, all washed down with a large milky coffee."

Emma didn't know whether to laugh, cry or race back to the sanctuary of her flat.

Barnaby continued, for this was not the first woman who had been in tears in front of him in any of his parishes, and he had experience in spades.

"There's a very simple explanation for the feel-good feeling of comfort food, well, perhaps it's not quite so simple. It's all to do with foods that have lots of carbohydrates in them. They trigger the release of weird things called neurotransmitters like serotonin, the feel-good transmitter. This can improve the mood and sense of well-being, temporarily. On the other hand, perhaps chips and gravy, or baked beans in my case, could be related to really good childhood memories, a lovely chunk of nostalgia. Or maybe it's just a pleasurable and distracting activity that takes my mind off the sadness. Who knows? All I do know is that every time I eat happy grub, I have to let my belt out another notch!"

By this time Emma was under his spell, she was captivated. She knew exactly what he was doing by rabbiting on and giving her time to compose herself. She turned away and blew her nose loudly just as Mollie placed the teacakes between them, exactly as ordered with lashings of butter.

Next came the tea and Barnaby poured for both of them. With an upset woman, while serving the tea, history had taught him not to insensitively use the age old saying of, 'Shall I be mother, then?' just in case.

Emma looked at him and decided he meant well.

"Did I ever tell you the story of when I was administering at a funeral at my last parish?" rambled on Barnaby. "Well, there were lots of people there but especially three brothers at their father's graveside. The eldest was a teacher who said to the other two, 'Dad loaned me some money when I started working all those years ago and I never repaid him. I feel really bad about it'. So, with that he threw a £20 note into the grave and said, 'I feel so much better now'. The middle son, a painter and decorator, said he also owed his father £20 for ladders and paint to set up his business and he too threw a £20 note into the grave. Immediately, he said he too felt better now his debt to his father had been paid. The third son, an accountant, said he also owed his father £20. With that he climbed into the grave, collected the two £20 notes and put them in his pocket. He wrote a cheque for £60, left it on the coffin and climbed out."

"No! Is that true?" asked Emma wide eyed. "Honestly?"

"Absolutely. As true as my name is Barnaby Hooligan Fitzwallerby Crump... the third."

Emma looked at him and smiled. Composed now thanks to the distraction, she put her hand on his sleeve and whispered, "Thank you."

"My pleasure." He smiled in return.

Mollie, who had also been listening to the story, leaned over them while clearing the cups and plates and in a very perplexed tone said, "But Barnaby, I don't understand. How will the dead father be able to cash the cheque?

Barnaby chucked and said, "Oh, Mollie, it's such a good job you're pretty." All three laughed out loud. "And the same again please, Mollie," he called through their laughter as she headed back to the kitchen.

Shortly after, Mollie brought more tea and currant buns, laughed again at the comment, said goodnight to them both and discreetly left.

Now that Barnaby and Emma were alone, he continued. "Sometimes it's just not your turn." He paused. "Sometimes you have to miss a turn. Sometimes you are told to pass go, but you do not collect £200. It all seems so unfair at the time, but your turn will come, I promise you." Barnaby was talking slowly but with great empathy. "One day it will definitely be your turn, but just not today. And there may be many good reasons for that. Providence may have decided you're not quite ready, just yet."

Emma sat, not saying anything, but hanging on his every word.

Barnaby continued, a little louder. He was coming alive and gesturing with both of his hands as he said, "When we visualise the future for ourselves, we draw it in our minds eye with brightly coloured crayons, big stars, bright sunshine, glitter and popcorn. We visualise our future through rainbow glasses and hear bells, bird song and music. But life's not like that." And then he spoke really quietly, "We're not in charge, Emma. We think we are, but the one thing this job has taught me is that we definitely are not." Then he returned to his normal speaking voice, "But on the positive side, maybe Providence has a bigger and more realistic plan for you, a plan coloured in more lustrous and radiant colours than you could ever imagine. A plan where love and kindness are the main players. But before she can share that plan, she must ensure that whoever is chosen is well prepared for the biggest challenge of their lives, whatever that is. I promise you that Providence won't let your plan or your special chance pass you by. You just need to trust her. She has been doing it a very long time and looking back on all of the lives that I've come into contact with, she knew what she was doing, every time."

Emma was in awe of him as he spoke, as if she was sitting in the front pew as a little girl. She listened as though he was in her mind. He was right. Everything he said was right. But how could he have possibly known the result of the test? And was she ready to be a mother or not?

"Before you ask me how I could possibly know what's wrong, let me assure you that I don't, for sure. But having been a vicar for a long time, I can guarantee when a woman in her thirties is as distressed as you are, it can be only one of three things. One: anxiety over money? Well, I think *Crumpets* is going a storm, so it's probably not money."

Emma shook her head and sniffed. "No, it's not money."

"Two: a relationship problem?"

Here Emma was not so confident. She shrugged her shoulders, saying neither saying yes or no and didn't meet his gaze.

"Or three: a baby thing?"

Emma's eyes filled with tears and he handed her a clean handkerchief.

Barnaby nodded and continued, "One of the things that Providence may have been withholding from you came to me recently and it may well influence your decision about whether now is a good time to start a family or not. It's been haunting me now for weeks. I needed the right time to broach the subject. I also believe we have become friends and in no way do I want to damage that relationship. However, when I first met your Dave, I was sure I'd seen him before. I recalled I had married a man just like him eight years ago in my last parish. I've kept records and photos of all the people I've married, so I checked. Now I'm sure; I married him to a young Irish nurse who'd become pregnant."

Emma took a large intake of breath, put her hand over her mouth and shut her eyes tightly, wanting to hide from hearing any more.

Barnaby spoke gently, "They had a little boy but his wife hated living in England and returned home to Dublin, with the little boy, to be with her mother. I can't find any record of them divorcing. I'm so sorry to be the bearer of this news, but I believe Providence wants you to know that your Dave is already married. Only a real friend would tell you something as devastating as this."

Emma shook her head back and forth, not believing it could be true. "No, no, no," she said, through her tears.

"There must be a host of other things that he's done since you've been together. Maybe insignificant on their own or perhaps didn't quite make sense at the time so you dismissed them, but now there is an underlying explanation. They will all slot into place, whether you want them to or not."

Barnaby waited for the bombshell to settle.

Emma nodded as she remembered the 'important client' that Dave had to go to Dublin regularly to meet. Things that he *had* to post to clients. Night time calls that he cut short when she walked into the room. Plus, a host of other signs, inconsequential on their own, but now...

"What should I do?" she asked.

"Nothing until you have the whole story. Now do you understand why Providence doesn't believe it's the right time for you?"

Barnaby poured some more tea and spread butter on his now cold teacake. "That was the most upsetting information you could ever have had from Providence, but there is a much brighter piece of news."

Emma looked up at him quizzically. What could possibly balance out what she had just heard?

"There is someone close to you who would give up everything just for a smile from you. But you've missed the signs because you've been too busy. You have lost sight of your 'slow down and feel the vibes around you' button. Someone has already given up all their dreams just to stay close to you. Your blindness comes from your fear of taking on any more challenges in your life at the moment. However, I believe he would make you very happy."

Barnaby put his hand on Emma's arm and held it gently. He said, "Just don't let him go."

Emma looked at him questioningly, her mind racing through all the white-van-drivers, her customers and friends, not understanding, not trusting.

"Now, on a completely new subject, can I be perfectly frank with you, Emma?" She nodded, believing there could be nothing else he could possibly say that would have any more impact than what had been said so far. "Your two friends Arthur and Martha..." Emma's eyes opened wide with surprise. "They are such delightful spirits, but they have no need to keep a watchful eye on me, thank you. I am protected by a much higher order."

She held her hand over her mouth to conceal her guilty smile, amazed that he knew of their existence

"How long have you known?"

"Ever since," he confirmed.

"Sorry, Barnaby," apologised Emma. She slowly buttered her cold teacake and took a big bite, letting her brain catch up with the conversation. She eventually said, "While we are being honest with each other, may I tell you something Lillian has shared with me, about her fears about you? She is a devout Christian and is building a formidable case against you."

"Lillian has nothing to fear from me. I think she may be a little bumfuzzled. Has it anything to do with my stone pillar?"

"Yes. She sees it as a graven image."

"Graven image!" he exclaimed. "Good grief." It was his turn now to be put on the spot. He needed several moments to consider his reply.

"The stone erected in my garden is in the centre of the place I go to pray. A special place. It is not some graven image. It is *my* place, *my* sanctuary, *my* piece of heaven. It was hewn from the hills behind the miner's cottage in which I was born. I was brought up in a tiny Welsh village and my first language is Welsh, so I pray in Welsh. The stone was transported here and erected by friends from my childhood. It makes me feel at home. I sensed Lillian behind me in the garden the other day but I had no idea she would reach a 'graven image' conclusion. She has quite the vivid imagination." Barnaby shook his head.

"She thought you were speaking in tongues."

Barnaby raised his thick dark eyebrows. "I think the Welsh Language Society would have something to say about confusing God's own beautiful, musical language Welsh with speaking in tongues."

"What about honouring your mother and father? She heard you shouting on the phone the other day."

"I love my mother and father more than life itself, but my mother is suffering from early signs of dementia and my father is going deaf. I want them to make the move into supported accommodation now while they understand the benefits, rather than me make the decisions for them in a few years. If they wait, the move would be shrouded in confusion and I would be blamed. I want to help them decide but there are times when I just can't help them understand." He shook his head in frustration.

"What about not coveting your neighbour's wife – Nancy?"

"Aha, I can understand Lillian's concerns there for I have been tested and sadly, found wanting. I failed the test and I am ashamed of myself but I don't know what to do about it. I am in torment. Trust me, I'm wracked with guilt. I hoped I could keep it a secret." He shrugged. "I'm just a man."

"I'm not sure there is much secrecy there for even I've heard the chit chat here in *Crumpets* about the attention you've paid Nancy recently," chided Emma.

"Well, before you ask, no, I have not committed adultery. But I came damn close the other night. I blame Arthur for his candlelight intervention. You can tell him his timing could not have been better or worse depending on your standpoint. And before you ask about 'thou shalt not kill', I have no plans to kill anyone, however, some members of the dominoes and mothball brigade are working their way up the list bloody fast." Barnaby banged his fist on the table top to emphasise the point.

Emma smiled. "Thank you for tonight. You're right, I need time to become more grounded before I start a family just for me, which would be for all the wrong reasons."

Barnaby nodded at her admission.

"Also, I can confirm with Lillian that you are 'nearly' a thoroughly decent vicar from all your explanations."

Barnaby returned her smile and covered her hands with his.

"And you, Emma, have made me confront the biggest question I will ever be faced with in my life. Perhaps, after all the years I have put into vicaring, it is now *my* time."

# CHAPTER 21

Twelve months after Emma and Barnaby's enlightening conversation, the first Bucket Street wedding in years took place between a very contented butcher and the owner of a cafe called *Crumpets*. The ceremony was conducted by, who else than, the local parish vicar, Barnaby Clifton.

The whole street was festooned in flags and bunting. Even the white-van-drivers decorated their vans for the occasion and formed a procession to take the bride and guests to church. Jumbo and Bean gave Emma away and Mollie was maid of honour. The wedding breakfast was held in *Crumpets*, of course.

———

Dave finally confessed his secret family to Emma after she confronted him about it. After guiltily packing up everything, he slinked away to Ireland to fulfil his obligations as a husband and dad.

———

*Crumpets* continued to thrive. Its reputation had grown by the day due to its famous bacon cobs featuring in a local newspaper. So much so, a new bacon cob preparation area had been built in the tiny back yard.

———

Bucket Street became even more prosperous. A barber and a builders' merchant opened up close to the original three shops and all five were doing well.

———

Jumbo completed his apprenticeship and, to the delight of his parents, won a scholarship to continue studying at the engineering company. Lillian said a little prayer of thanks for all the time he had spent at *Crumpets*.

———

Bean completed his college course and left to pursue an exciting new venture on the cruise ships. He became an award-winning pastry chef but, eventually, he returned to Bucket Street to begin another adventure. However, he has not touched a drop of red wine since that fateful day.

———

Mollie continued to help at *Crumpets 1* until she began managing *Crumpets 2* on the other side of town, which included a bakery/patisserie section run by the award-winning pastry chef... Bean.

———

Nancy divorced her husband who admitted he had secretly been leading a life of two halves for several years.

———

Barnaby Clifton sadly moved away from the parish, finally driven out by the dominoes and mothball brigade, and the bishop who didn't want to upset the parishioners.

Nancy helped him pack up his few possessions and promptly sat in the removal van outside the vicarage refusing to move! She explained to him that he would need someone to help him settle into his new home and light all the candles. She also promised, "I will stay with you in case the candles ever do go out again, and if they do, I will never, ever let go of you!"

———

A very contrite Lillian, who had learned the painful lesson of jumping to conclusions, continued to clean the vicarage for the new vicar. The Reverend Shirley Bemrose-Smyth and her husband were keen gardeners but teetotal.

———

And the two spirits, Martha and Arthur, continued to live at 52 Bucket Street, just as they always had.

# ACKNOWLEDGEMENTS

My special thanks go to my editor-in-chief Claire Jennison, of C. L. Jennison Editorial, for all her patience, help and sensitive guidance.

Also to Colleen Capewell for her imaginative drawing of *Crumpets'* shop front.

And finally David Owen for his interpretation of the front cover.

# OTHER BOOKS BY
## HOWARD G AWBERY

Five Strange Tales

The Music Box

Me and My Lamp

The Odd Noble Deed

Isobelle

Five Even Stranger Tales

Five Coffee Time Tales

A Sprig of Mint

Don't Eat the Sandwiches!

Bethesda

# FIVE STRANGE TALES

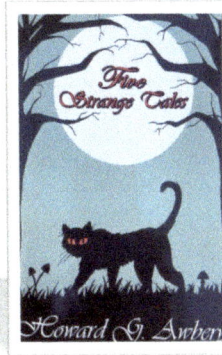

A cat with attitude, green-fingered garden gnomes, a Roman helmet, and two fiercely protective ghosts feature in this delightful anthology.

Each one of the *Five Strange Tales* has been written to accompany a cup of tea and a biscuit, whilst pleasantly disorientating the reader and challenging what they believe to be 'real' for a few moments.

When finished, the book will be lovingly replaced on the coffee table, leaving the reader smiling to themselves and wondering could that actually happen?

# THE MUSIC BOX

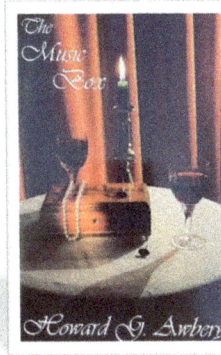

In 1938, with preparations for war well under way, newlyweds Celia and Carsten Prestwick begin their honeymoon on the night train to Scotland.

Sabotage, a steam train race, and two tangled love triangles are just some of the issues that tumble out of this intriguing romantic novel; a novel peppered with classic Howard G. Awbery twists and turns.

Readers will be able to put *The Music Box* down just once...at the very end!

# ME AND MY LAMP

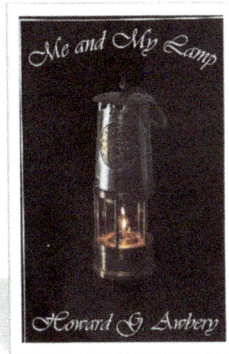

Dr Howard G. Awbery joined the British coal mining industry as a fresh faced eighteen-year-old and emerged thirty years later, battered and bruised but worldlier for the richness of the experience.

In this captivating book, *Me and My Lamp*, he recounts stories from those years. Stories of human kindness, national coal strikes, personal injury, a ghostly warning, and the eclectic family of miners who made him laugh, and cry.

As one of the few colliers left who once filled a 'stint' of coal using a shovel and set wooden props to secure the roof, he draws the reader into an underground world that those who have never ventured shudder to imagine. However, his world of coal was not a black world at all, for his mining stories depict a bright, colourful world, full of excitement, challenge, and amazing people.

# THE ODD NOBLE DEED

The Rangemore Hotel is a tired, Victorian hotel struggling to survive on the North Wales coastline. A coastline owned by the sea, loaned by the sea, and at any time, could be reclaimed by the sea.

Equally as unpredictable as the sea are the fortunes of the owners and staff of The Rangemore Hotel, the backdrop to *The Odd Noble Deed*.

Four people associated with this once grand hotel tumble and crash into each other's lives. Passion, treachery and lies leave only two winners.

Or are they winners? For to win, one must truly value the prize.

# ISOBELLE

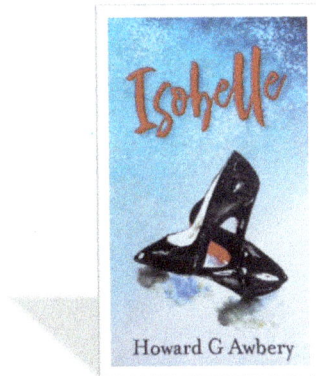

Never in a million years could Isobelle have imagined that any one customer would make so much difference to her life. One day, however, into her busy London boutique came such a customer. 'Shoulders' as she derogatorily referred to him, rocked her equilibrium and tumbled her settled, solitary, secure life over and over again.

Before 'Shoulders', Isobelle's independence was her armour against all-comers; she believed her life and emotions impenetrable. As she reluctantly became increasingly embroiled in this customer's complex life, she realised how wrong she was.

# FIVE EVEN STRANGER TALES

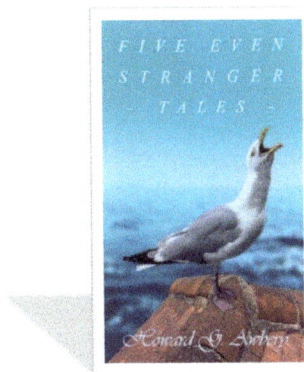

Howard G. Awbery has done it again. An intriguing follow-on from *Five Strange Tales*, *Five Even Stranger Tales* will not disappoint.

With your log burner blazing and a steaming cup of frothy, hot chocolate by your side, these creative and carefully crafted tales will keep you guessing until the final line.

Mix seagulls and weddings with philanthropy and a doctor's computer with a mind of its own, and you won't have any idea what's coming next.

Cantering through an eclectic gathering of characters, you will finally come to rest on an allotment in the company of a tramp called Humphrey. But all is not as it appears...

# FIVE COFFEE TIME TALES

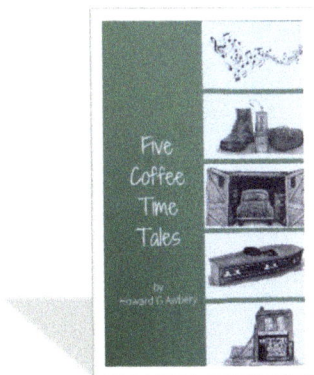

Definition: Special moments, planned for and dedicated to drinking coffee. Coffee time is instead of work, not with work, culminating in an 'ahrrrr' sound.

Planning for coffee time: Mobiles out of reach, frustrating Sudoku out of sight, to-do lists away, and who cares if imbroglio is a real word in today's crossword?

Adding joy: Only one thing can improve coffee time – a good book. Howard G. Awbery's *Five Coffee Time Tales* includes charming short stories, each with a 'Well, I really didn't expect that!' twist, to be read in the time it takes to drink a cup of coffee.

Enjoy your coffee.

# A SPRIG OF MINT

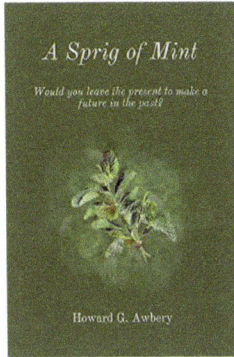

An interest in ancient stone circles keeps James, a financial trader in the city of London, well-grounded. When visiting a little-known stone circle in North Wales, on the summer solstice, he is transported back to the time of the circle's construction. James lives among the Late Bronze Age villagers, befriending the architect of the stone circle, Barnaby, and a young widow, Eira.

James rejoins the present, quickly realising he was far happier in the past than his current, shallow London life. He returns to the past only to find it under siege by the Hunllef, a warring, wandering tribe. Following a bloody battle he and Eira escape to the present.

Beth, a PhD student studying the history of stone circles, befriends James and Eira and becomes entangled in their lives spanning two time zones.

# DON'T EAT THE SANDWICHES!

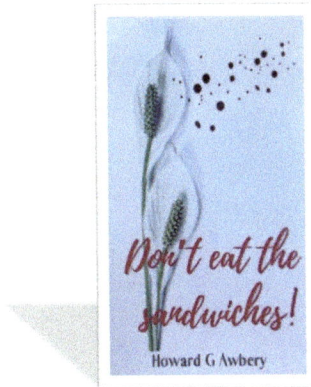

*Don't Eat the Sandwiches!* is a story set in 1975, of two cousins in their mid-thirties whose lives bounce back together.

Despite Joanne, an accountant by profession, vowing never, ever to go on holiday again with "Let's drink Malaga dry!" Veronica, she hears the announcement, "Ladies and gentlemen, please fasten your seat belts, we will shortly be landing at Costa del Sol airport."

Returning from their holiday peeling and poor, they hatch a late night gin and paella-fuelled plan. Sending Veronica to work in a care home seems the obvious source of new guests for Joanne's newly acquired, failing, funeral parlour.

However, providence has other ideas in this tale of comeuppance woven by Howard G. Awbery.

# BETHESDA

**BETHESDA**

*A sequel to 'Don't Eat the Sandwiches'*

*Howard G Awbery*

Bethesda Residential Home for the Active Elderly is well on her way to becoming the UK South Coast's Residential Home of First Choice, all thanks to her formidable managing director, Veronica Puxworthy.

For the past four years, since unexpectedly inheriting Bethesda in 1975, Veronica and her motley crew of managers have worked hard to make it a success. But now, after a series of surprise attacks, that success is under serious threat.

Can Veronica and her team—her cousin Joanne, an ex-convict and ex-accountant; Vincent, an ex-hearse driver with useful mates in the underworld; Elsie, Vincent's wife, a medium and ex-embalmer; Alejandro, a hot-tempered Spaniard and head chef; Rosie, Alejandro's naïve but sweet wife; and, finally, Godfrey, the quintessentially English, pipe-smoking, meticulous groundsman —overcome the unscrupulous attackers?

With a little help from an extraordinary source, they devise a plan to protect their beloved Bethesda. Can they save her from further attacks before it's too late?

Milton Keynes UK
Ingram Content Group UK Ltd.
UKHW020218151124
451096UK00021B/259

9 781835 634677